3:33a.m.

By Author: Dana B. Auer

"ISBN: 979-8-9887-6591-2"

Cover design by: Jenna Zimdars

Line /copy editors: Ann Weidner, John Kimmel

Back cover portrait: Gavin MCcue, gavinmccuephotography.pixieset.com

ACKNOWLEDGMENTS

Thank you to a long list of beta readers, for their time and encouragement.

Every writer needs the exceptional efforts of professional line and copy editors; thank you Ann Weidner and John Kimmel.

Jenna, what an awesome cover! Exactly as I imagined four years ago.

Mari and Rachel, you have my sincere gratitude. Your early efforts on my behalf were priceless.

I want to thank the many podcast hosts who continue teaching me about writing while driving in my semi, especially Savannah Gilbo, Emma Dhesi, and Kenny MacKay. Your podcasts were vital to writing a story that works, turning this reader into a writer, and allowing me to author my dream.

Thank you to Lauren Ranalli for your launch guidance.

I dedicate my love for the craft of writing to my sweet Mother, Esther, always my biggest hero and strongest encourager.

No less gratitude goes out to my beautiful wife, Jackie; her patience and understanding go without saying.

"Blind denial, an ordinary life choice, shared by the majority. Only a select few prepare for the unexpected."

By Dana B. Auer

Pure Crystal

August 9, 2026, 7:14 p.m.

Galesville, WI

Ace stood looking out the picture window of his four-season sunroom, struggling to relax. He couldn't remember the last time he noticed such a beautiful sunset. Shards of sunlight created an iridescent glow that exploded over the hillside. A well-known artist like Claude Monet would have struggled to capture the essence of this scene.

Unfortunately, it caused a glare that reflected directly onto his sixty-five-inch television screen. He and Ailyn worked together to close the blinds.

He sat down and started looking at their viewing choices; he rarely had control of the television remote. He could smell the freshly popped buttered popcorn, their television treat.

"What do you want to watch tonight?" He asked Ailyn.

"We could start a new season of "Alone."

Ace watched as the options slowly scrolled across the screen.

Ailyn reached down, picked up her snack bowl, and bumped the remote, accidentally interrupting the slow scroll across the screen, landing on the liberal-leaning show, 'The Sight.' Former First Lady Regina Putman was interviewed poolside via Zoom at her home in the Hamptons.

Women's voices came through out of the soundbar. "Honestly, I'm having a lot more fun not being in the White House, Blythe. I'm a little more relaxed here by my pool than in the Oval Office." They cackled in their mutual appreciation for each other and the luxuries in life.

"As long as we don't have to watch that witch, I don't care what we watch." Ace didn't like the Putmans, now evident as he suddenly changed positions inside the recliner. He didn't like their personalities or their policies. Their promotion of digital currency sacrificed most of his and Ailyn's retirement savings. They lost, while the Putmans and many in their political party became millionaires.

Ailyn, knowing better than to encourage further political conversation on a Sunday evening, resumed searching until settling on 'Alone' on the menu page. They both enjoyed the characters' resourcefulness as they worked to stay alive in adverse conditions. Watching people survive and sometimes even thrive.

****

The Hamptons were very beautiful at this time of year.

Warm August air from the coast wisped gently past Regina's flushed cheeks. Smiling, she thought her interview went very well.

After she and her husband lost the last presidential race, the paid publicity was almost better for Regina's image. Now that they were out of public office, she had more opportunities to manipulate what the country saw and heard about her.

She pushed the green answer button when the satellite phone began vibrating on the glass tabletop.

"Regina Putman."

"Yes, hello, Sheik. Everything is ready on my end."

"Have you received the AI program's default password?"

"Yes, it will give your people shared control over the Space Force satellite system."

"Living like a queen sounds great to me."

"Then everything appears to be in order. I wish I could be there to watch Pruett's face!"

"Okay, you too."

The satellite phone went silent; she reached down and placed it back on the table.

Two dutiful armed guards stood stoically at the pool's entrance. Both men have been in the Putman service detail since her husband's term in office. Regina strategically hand-picked them herself.

"Are the helicopters ready? President Putman and I must be in the air before eight tomorrow."

"Yes, ma'am, everything's ready for departure."

"Thank you, Morris."

"Alex, we're going on a trip tomorrow, dear," walking toward the jacuzzi, she reached out and pushed through the glass doorway; exhilaration overcame her body. Power and control gave her a dopamine rush, even better than how she'd felt on the campaign trail. She relished every second.

"Oh, yeah. Where to this time?"

"We'll be staying at Stein's place for a while."

"Oh, really? I like spending time there." Alex reached down indiscreetly and adjusted himself in his chair.

"Make sure you pack everything you want to take with you. We're leaving at 8am."

Alex Putman set down his phone; he'd spent the morning scrolling through porn. It was a full-time job to keep up with everything new on the dark web. "Okay, I'll go work on it now."

Regina walked toward him, noticing the bulge in her husband's swim trunks; she shook her head and smiled. "I bet you will."

The now elderly couple have long practiced an erotic lifestyle suitable for an open marriage. It started in college when fun and pleasure in the late seventies preceded studies and academia. It suited Regina; she could be ambitious and use sex to her advantage and not be beholden to her husband; he was also free to explore his options. It was a marriage of convenience.

Alex walked toward the kitchen. “I’m hungry! Maybe Maria can help me find something to satisfy my appetite?”

Regina shook her head at him again and reached inside her Coach satchel, a brand-new cellphone in hand, still in its plastic package. Her staff signed NDAs about everything that happened in their home. Her team's future needs were never a top priority.

“It’s Regina. Is everything ready for tomorrow morning?”

“Good; you can reach me on my satellite phone when it’s all done.”

“He’s not going to know what hit him.”

“Yes, by then, it will be too late.”

“You can join us on the island when it’s safe.”

“Yeah, it will be nice not having to play all these games anymore. We can all be together again.”

“I can’t wait to see you too! Be careful. Bye.”

She danced her way over to a beverage tray by the fireplace and reached for a crystal lowball, lifted the ice bucket lid, and dropped two cubes into the Waterford glass, the unmistakable chime of quality. Bombay Sapphire flowed smoothly from the bottle, covering the ice around the glass. “Here’s to a long hard fight, Bob. It’s been nice knowing you!” The words were spoken quietly from her lips as she raised the glass and took a hearty sip. The crisp juniper and citrus liquid woke her senses and reminded her of her mission.

Sounds of pleasure came from the kitchen.

****

The next day, Regina sent her bags to the car.

“Are you ready to go, Alex?”

“I think so. I’m sure I can send someone back to get anything I may have forgotten.”

“It’s going to be a while before we can return here,

Alex."

"Why's that, Regina? What's going on? What have you done?"

"Don't worry about it, dear. We can talk about that later. Just trust me."

The couple stepped up onto the helicopter steps and climbed aboard. They were in the air, heading south inside the demarcation lines of the coastline.

When the power grid went down, Regina watched as the lights on the buildings along the shore went dark, unusual in the early sunrise.

As they rose to a higher elevation, multiple smoke plumes rose from the western horizon line as tactical nuclear weapons detonated onto designated military targets along the East Coast.

Closing her eyes, she imagined President Robert "Bob" Pruett's face and played the tape through to the end. The explosion, seeing his body hurled backward. His death, the destruction.

Alex looked out the helicopter window. "What have you done, Regina?" The look on his face was in shock and disbelief, and he was shaking his head.

Once again, she just smiled.

Freeze, Flee, or Fight

Day 1 (3:33 a.m.)

Galesville, WI

"Errr, errr, errr, errr!"

Ace's eyes flew open.

The red number, 3:33, shined bright on the ceiling above him. A soft glow from the moon illuminated the room. He reached out from under the blankets to stop the alarm and unplug his smartphone.

He'd been journaling his dreams since 1998, a hobby that became a habit. He took a moment and wrote what he remembered down on a tablet from his nightstand.

8/11/2026: I was playing chess. The room was full of people eating sweet bread and whispering in an unfamiliar language. The other man's fingers were on top of the black king, and he called me Governor.

It was another of those mornings with a twelve-hour workday scheduled. At sixty-four, days of 'jumping' out of bed were long over. Decades of construction work had taken a heavy toll. It took an effort not to let it show. The first morning steps were a little slow and careful.

The bathroom mirror was a sobering reminder of the fight to stay young, accomplishing the mundane task of shaving his bald head with an electric razor, a white goatee, long again, almost to his chest.

He walked down the hall to the kitchen, looking at a picture of his family. Pride rushed over him; he knew he and his wife had raised their two children, Hatty and Reese, well.

Ailyn, his spouse of forty-two years, always set up the coffee maker the night before. The smell of breakfast blend filled his nostrils as the coffee beans finished percolating. It was the comfort of habit, routine and lifelong love.

Making his lunch and packing his cooler with various healthy foods, he believed that food was fuel and quality fuel was an essential part of aging well.

"Ailyn," he said, "I had the strangest dream last night that I was the Governor." He often experienced premonition dreams or replied early to something Ailyn was just thinking. He credited his grandmother with sharing her gift.

Ailyn stopped her husband's explanation mid-paragraph. She had listened to many of these descriptive dream stories before. "Wait. Tell me all about it tonight, okay? I'm going downstairs to work out. Gimme a kiss!"

"Okay, I'll see you later. Love you."

"Love you too. Be safe."

****

Ace watched the garage door close in the rearview mirror as he drove down the cement driveway to the street.

After fourteen years with his current employer, he often wished he had driven a semi right after graduation from high school. It could have made early retirement possible. His personal decisions led him down a different road.

The twenty-three-mile drive felt the same as it had last Friday. Depending on commercial breaks or his stops at the Trip Quick convenience store, the commute usually took about four to five songs. He pushed the fourth pre-set on the radio, a classic rock station, and he sang along to "Riding the Storm Out" by REO Speedwagon.

La Crosse, Wisconsin, hadn't changed since he and Ailyn moved to the area in 1991 from the state's eastern side. But the moral standard had. People used to act like they lived in small-town Wisconsin. The appeal of the city slowly deteriorated. Like most major metro zones, it's became colder and less personable. Since the political division in 2016 involving former President Mrung, people seldom looked each other in the eye anymore.

Ace wasn't the first employee to arrive at the Redi mix plant that morning. It was early, but the office light was already on. Entry through the service door required dual authentication-punching a three-digit code into a lockbox and then using a hidden key to gain access.

He punched his time card at 4:57 a.m. and dropped it back

into his slot. Walking out to his semi, his first load of Portland cement powder was due in Black River Falls, Wisconsin, by 7:00 a.m.

****

Arriving at the concrete plant, the parking lot was chaotic with movement. Flashing red and yellow lights reflected off the steel siding. One of the cement mixers was under the chute, its drum turning fast while filling. Several other mixers were in position, waiting their turn.

Dexter, another powder hauler, had just finished unloading his tanker. Passing him in the dusty driveway as they greeted each other with a wave and a nod. He had a familiar and yet, peculiar feeling. Had he just experienced another deja vu?

Backing up a pneumatic tanker is comparable to pushing a brontosaurus backward. Negotiating almost 80,000 pounds toward a cement silo demanded one's complete concentration.

Styx's "Crystal Ball" played on the radio. It stopped, replaced with dead air.

An agitated voice came on, followed by the sound of rustling papers.

"This is Mike Haise, coming to you live from the WISM newsroom. We have some breaking news just in." The announcer cleared his throat and continued in a shaky voice. "A suicide bomber has just attacked President Pruett in Washington, DC. I'll update you as more information comes in, but that's all we know right now. Stay tuned here with me on WISM 1490 AM, 93.2 FM."

As the music started again. Ace stopped his truck short of the silo, yanking out the tractor brake, feeling a whirlwind of emotions. He remembered sitting on his mother's lap as an infant. She had watched as President Kennedy was shot and killed on live television, seen on her black and white Zenith television. The uncomfortable feelings of fear and sadness returned.

Climbing out of the cab and running to the office. The loud sounds of the turning drum on the Redi mix truck and fast-moving conveyor belts delivering gravel and sand to the mixing plant barely registered in his mind. He threw open the dirty office door and shouted. "Did you guys hear what just happened?"

John, a co-worker, replied. "Yeah, Greg has it up on the computer."

"I gotta go call my wife." Ace closed the office door behind him and ran back to his truck to his phone plugged into a holder on the dashboard. "Call Ailyn," he ordered by voice command. He'd often wondered if something like this could happen following the last five election cycles.

"Dan!" Ailyn answered. "Oh my God, did you hear the news? Where are you?" Her tone was one of worry; she only used his given name when she was distraught or angry.

Ace replied. "I'm in Black River. I just heard it on the radio! I'm going to try to get all my loads done. Hopefully, nothing else will happen. But if it does, I'll meet you at the house."

"Nothing else is going to happen," she said, but her words rang hollow.

"Ailyn, somebody just tried to assassinate President Pruett."

Ace had paid close attention to the many governments mixed messages and strange narratives to comfort, distract and create conflict within the population, knowing they were masking their true intentions. Ace watched the lies and saw the plots. He had a deep distrust—bordering on paranoia—combined with his ever-present survivalist instinct. Unlike most of the population, including Ailyn, it gave him a different view of trust in the world. It put him into protection mode.

"Everyone's stopped working," Ailyn responded uncomfortably. "They're watching the news on their computers. I hope nothing else happens. Dan, what about the kids?"

"They're probably wondering what will happen next, just like us. Did you try to call them yet?"

"Yeah, but I can't get through. I keep getting a busy signal."

"I'm going back into the office to see if there's any more news; I'll call you back in a few minutes."

"Okay. Call me right back."

Ace spoke to his phone. "Call Hatty," but he also got a busy signal. The same happened when he tried to call Reese.

The phone's screen changed when Ace unplugged it. He slipped it into his shirt pocket and opened the plant's office door. All his coworkers stood around Greg, looking over his shoulder at the computer screen.

"Ace, can you believe this?" Dennis asked, pointing a gloved finger at the monitor.

"What else happened?" Ace asked. He was already anticipating more details.

Greg moved aside and turned up the volume on his computer.

"It's pure chaos in Washington, DC, and many other major cities across the eastern half of the country. Massive explosions are causing widespread panic throughout the United States. We do not know who is behind these calculated attacks. No group, person, or country has claimed responsibility. Thousands of innocent citizens and government officials are presumed dead. Emergency rescue efforts are underway. Vice President Baylor has declared martial law nationwide. Every available National Guard member, please report to your duty stations. As of this time, all military bases are on red alert. All emergency personnel, please report to your designated stations. Stay tuned for further up..."

The monitor went black, and the office went dark. Greg sat back and raised his arms in the air. "I didn't do it. It wasn't me!" Ace happened to glance down at his wristwatch. It was 7:12 a.m.

"Holy shit, did the grid just go down?" Cody asked, looking surprised before laughing uncomfortably.

"No cell service, either." Ace held the button on the top of his phone. The screen was dark. He pushed it again, and the phone came back on. He knew an electromagnetic pulse couldn't have caused this. All the truck's diesel engines outside would have shut down.

"Greg, check the landline."

"Dead. That's weird." Greg hung up the receiver.

"What do we do now?" Jake asked, looking to his manager, Greg, for instruction.

"Go outside and see if the streetlights are on across the highway. Cody, go dump that load and wash your drum out."

The civil defense siren blared in the distance. Less than a minute later, Jake reported back. "No street lights are on by the furniture store."

Ace knew the concrete plant couldn't operate without electricity, phones, or internet service. They had no way to communicate with the main office, customers, or their families. This event disrupted their day.

"I don't know what to do," Greg said. "Hopefully, whatever's happening will get straightened out." He looked unnerved and unsure of what to do next. His crew waited.

Ace spoke up. "Right before the power went down, they said Vice President Baylor placed the country under martial law, I don't know about you guys, but I'm going home."

"Okay. Yeah, Ace is right. Punch out, you guys, and go home to your families." Greg combed his hands through his hair—a sign of his growing frustration.

"The time clock doesn't work without power," John said after several failed attempts.

"Just write in your times," Greg responded.

Ace turned to him. "I'm going to unhook and deadhead back in my semi."

"No. You should drive with me, Ace. Leave your truck up here. I'll still need the powder when everything gets back to normal. We can go to the main office in La Crosse and talk to Brad and Shan. You can drive your car home from there." Greg seemed to be hanging onto false hope.

Anxious and a little confused, Ace reluctantly agreed. "I'll go shut down my truck and grab my stuff."

Greg yelled from behind his desk, "Ace, I'll meet you by my truck!"

He opened the driver-side door and turned off the ignition key; his hand reached over to the handles of a get-home bag and a lunch box on the passenger seat. Doing this reminded him of a social media post over the weekend. Many of his friends and family lived in a comfortable state of denial. Only casual preppers carried bug-out bags.

Greg waited for Ace in his white company truck. Ace's coworkers sped through the open gate at the end of the driveway, kicking up dust on their way out.

"Hey Greg, should we take a gas can with us just in case?"

"No. Why? I just filled the tank this morning."

Greg had been a dedicated employee for over thirty years, planning for retirement at the end of this month.

"My phone's still not working," Ace said. "Check yours!" Conceding defeat, he placed his phone inside his bag's front pocket and zipped it closed.

Greg said. "No bars. Let's just go."

Ace switched on the stereo; there was nothing but static and dead air. He pushed the scan button to search for signals, but nothing came in on AM or FM. "Whatever blew the power knocked out all the radio stations, too." He and Greg looked at each other, bewildered. Facing the sunrise, Greg slowed for the stop sign, turned onto Hwy 54, and headed west toward the city. They saw the flashing blue lights of emergency vehicles near the freeway. The authorities blocked all ramps; traffic came to a sudden stop.

"What should we do now?" Greg asked.

"Turn around before we get stuck here."

"Oh, no!" Greg yelled.

In his rear-view mirror, he saw a vehicle coming fast at them and braced for impact. Ace turned and saw a blue Jeep Cherokee ricochet off a nearby minivan and smashed sideways into their truck box at near highway speed.

The collision caused both airbags to deploy and pushed the truck into oncoming traffic. Several cars swerved to avoid hitting them. Traffic was halted in both lanes now. The emergency civil defense sirens were still sounding just past the freeway, and police and fire sirens were everywhere.

"Are you okay?" Greg was shaken up from the collision. Ace jumped out of the truck and walked around to inspect it. The rear tire was flat, and the body panels of the truck box were damaged beyond repair. The vehicle was no longer drivable.

Opening the driver side door, Ace grabbed Greg's arm. "Come on, Greg. I'll help you, buddy." Greg was in a minor state of shock. Ace grabbed him by the shoulders and shook him gently, "Listen to me. We're going to be alright!"

Greg snapped out of it and shook it off, "Yeah, I'm okay. What do we do now?"

Ace was frustrated but stayed calm. This was their only way home. With no cell phone service, they had no way to reach out and ask anyone for help. Ailyn's face flashed quickly through his head. He was determined to meet her at home.

"We need to find a different vehicle."

The stunned Jeep driver got out of her vehicle. Her airbags had deployed and steam was escaping from under the crumbled hood; she was noticeably shaken but didn't appear hurt. Others also got out of their vehicles. Ace noticed an older bluish-gray Honda Ridgeline sitting in the westbound lane pulling two blue and white moto-cross bikes on a trailer. There was a large group gathered about fifty yards up the road in front of the Americana Hotel; the occupants of the

Ridgeline had joined them.

Ace had been a Good Samaritan for most of his life. He served others in times of crisis. This felt different. His survival instincts were strong, and he felt the pull to reunite with Ailyn—no matter the risk or cost. He was conflicted. Like many people around the globe, he and Ailyn got through the COVID-19 pandemic. They practiced social distancing methods, almost to the point of isolation. This experience definitely sharpened his fleeing instinct—or fight, if necessary.

"Greg, can you ride a dirt bike?"

"Yeah, I've ridden but it's been a long time. Why?"

Ace moved forward with his plan; he opened his backpack, pulled out a holstered Ruger 9-millimeter pistol, and hooked it over his belt. This was his concealed carry weapon since the law changed in Wisconsin. As always, he hoped he wouldn't have to use it.

He quickly readjusted some of the lunch box items and took a quick drink from his plastic water bottle.

"Come on, Greg. Let's go," he said as he swung his bag over his shoulder.

Ace led Greg to the trailer. On his way, he thought of his daughter, Hatty, and some of their survivalist conversations. He wondered if she and Reese were okay. He said a quick prayer for their safety and looked forward to calmer times. His mind turned back to the dirt bikes. There were no other viable options. He needed to get home and take care of his wife and family. He needed to stay focused.

The two Yamaha dirt bikes were strapped tightly into place. "One down and four up is the shifting pattern," Ace told Greg, who had followed him to the back of the trailer.

"What? Really, Ace? Are you nuts?" Greg backpedaled, shocked. "We don't even know what's happened yet."

"Greg, shit's hit the fan. I'm not going to stand here and try to convince you. Do you want to make it back home or not?" He saw the apprehension in Greg's eyes. "Okay. I'll go without you then."

"No, you're right. Let's do it!" Greg said. He was still shaking his head.

Ace climbed onto the trailer, stood between the two bikes, and split the straps with his pocket knife. He laid the bikes down gently on their sides, against the steel rail of the trailer.

Ace felt superhuman strength from deep inside, lifting each bike over the trailer rail, and setting them down on the ground.

"Hey!" Ace, looked up to see the owner of the Ridgeline running toward him. "Hey, stop!"

Greg grabbed one of the bikes and backed it up, pointing it the opposite way. He looked back to see Ace pull his pistol out of its holster and fire two shots into the air. The two approaching men darted for cover behind a vehicle.

Ace and Greg hopped onto the bikes. With two quick kicks, Ace's bike came to life.

Greg took off first, raising the front tire from popping the clutch too fast. Ace spun a half donut in the gravel. He'd been riding motorcycles since his early teens. An arched spray of rocks flew toward the bikes' former owners.

The crowd had panicked from the gunfire. This gave Ace and Greg time to power-shift down the ditch away from the congestion and chaos.

Ace knew they would need gas to make it home. Even if these bikes tanks were full, they may not make it home. He headed back to the concrete plant.

"What are you doing?" Greg yelled.

"Gas cans!"

****

"I filled both cans, Ace, and found some ratchet straps," Greg smiled uncomfortably as he and Ace strapped the cans to the seats.

"I haven't stolen anything since I was a kid, Ace. It doesn't feel very good." Ace was busy checking and rechecking supplies as well as mapping out the best routes home.

Ace rechecked his phone. "I still don't have any service. How about you?"

"Nope," Greg replied. "No bars. We usually have at least three here at the plant."

They shared a common goal; making it home to their families, no matter the cost. They both had made a serious commitment-unsure what would happen next. Would they face charges for stealing the bikes? The depth of the catastrophe they faced conflicted with the feeling that things would return to normal in a day or two. But Ace's gut told him that 'normal' wouldn't ever feel the same.

"Have you ever ridden the ATV and snowmobile trails down to the bridge by Melrose?" Ace asked.

"Yeah. About fifteen years ago."

"I think we should follow the railroad tracks down to Warrens and then ride the snowmobile trail to Cataract. We can get to the bridge on 108 from there."

"Okay, sounds good. I can't think of any other way to get across the river unless we try to go through town."

Ace shook his head, "No. Let's stay away from people as best we can." He knew things would get worse.

Please Stay Calm

Day 1, 7:26 a.m.

Onalaska, WI

The third floor of the regional medical center's Support Service building buzzed with the sounds of its employees. Ailyn's co-workers scattered into small groups discussing the President's assassination attempt and the power loss. No one was able to work without an Internet connection.

She was employed by a regional healthcare system that had installed a landfill gas generator powered by methane gas piped in from the La Crosse Landfill and rooftop solar panels so the buildings could maintain power. The entire hospital's operating system relied on renewable energy resources.

"I don't have phone service; do you have any bars?" Ailyn asked her closest work friend.

Connie looked down at her screen. "Nope. Me either."

"Wow, look at the freeway," Ailyn said. Their 3rd story office windows overlooked Interstate 90. Traffic was stopped in both directions.

"Do you see any accidents?" Ailyn asked.

Stranded drivers looked like busy ants from their vantage point. People were moving in and around their vehicles—some panicked and ran to fence lines along the sides of the highway.

Five large military trucks with giant V-shaped plows drove down the center of the westbound lane without regard for vehicle occupancy. The lead plow truck forced an opening like the key blocker on the front line of a quarterback sneak play. A caravan of smaller military trucks followed in single file behind them.

"What is the Army doing?" Connie asked, shocked. "Hey everybody, come here and look at this!" Metal-on-metal screeches could be heard through the office windows. The last V-plow turned left onto the gravel maintenance turnaround. It cleared all obstructions to the fence in front of the hospital buildings, then backed up and continued to follow behind the caravan.

A Humvee drove up to the steel border fence lining the freeway ditch and pushed it down. Employees started running to the elevators and stairs, while others stood frozen, watching the military actions in disbelief.

Two armored personnel carriers followed the Humvee over the fence and across the side road. They parked on the lawn between the Support Service and Clinic buildings.

Soldiers dispersed into two groups. Six fully armed men rushed to the front of the Support Service Building where Ailyn and Connie worked. The others marched to the entrances of the larger Onalaska Clinic.

"This doesn't look good at all." Ailyn's stomach churned. We've gotta get out of here right now, or we're going to get stuck here." She saw soldiers stop vehicles and force people to abandon their cars, making them go back inside the buildings.

"We can't go anywhere in our cars," Connie stated.

Ailyn whispered, "Go get your purse and anything else you need from your desk and meet me by my cubicle."

Right now, clear thinking was necessary. Chaos and confusion overshadowed their situation.

Ailyn dumped her carry bag onto the desk. She restocked it with valuable items: a wallet, lunch, and a half-empty bag of miniature candy bars. She also added a small travel tissue packet, a small bottle of hand sanitizer, and a paper pad with two pens.

"Connie, let's go," Ailyn insisted.

They hustled toward the rear stairway the two had descended together hundreds of times—a great exercise alternative to the elevator. Going down the three flights of stairs was easier today. They felt the urgency and purpose of their situation.

A crowd was packed into the front lobby, trying to get outside. Above the background noise, an amplified voice projected toward the building. "Stay calm. The country is now under martial law. Please stay inside the building until further notice."

The soldier's voice changed in tone and pitch; he demanded. "We need your cooperation. Go back into your building." The sounds of emergency sirens filled the air.

A group of employees rushed out the door through a small squad in front of the building. A uniformed officer fired a quick three-second burst into the air. "Stop," he yelled.

The screaming crowd scattered again. Some returned to the crowded office building's entrance. Ailyn could see through the office windows on the first floor that a few employees kept running toward the parking lot.

"Let's go out the maintenance doors." Ailyn pushed open the hallway door and ran toward the exit sign, pulling Connie with her. She pushed open the heavy steel door and emerged into the bright sunlight. Ailyn squinted at her wristwatch. She wondered what Dan would be doing right now.

"C'mon," Ailyn whispered. "I need to grab something out of my car."

The parking lots and the road between their office building and the clinic were jammed with running automobiles.

Hidden behind her vehicle, Ailyn opened the rear passenger door and grabbed the pack. She watched three soldiers run to the doors they had just exited, herding people back into the building.

"Ailyn, where are we going?"

"Just trust me, okay?" Ailyn grabbed Connie's hand and yanked her down to the pavement as one of the soldiers looked over his shoulder to see who was talking.

Snaking their way through the parked cars, they eventually reached the back of the parking lot. Natural prairie grass separated asphalt from the tree line.

Ailyn looked once more at their building and stepped over the edge of the grassy bank. Here it smelled of nature instead of heavy exhaust fumes. They pushed sideways through the dense brush and away from the other soldiers fanning out. through the parking lot, collecting people from their cars. No one followed. No one saw.

They edged down a steep embankment to the bottom of the hill, stepping out of the trees and standing on the jagged edge of the grassy marshland.

Ailyn thought of her husband; he told her that in an emergency, she should avoid people. Though no one was near the open marshland, she felt exposed. She led Connie back into cover; they continued to walk along the edge of the woods, coming to a clearing behind an assisted living facility.

Once again, they were forced into the open, crossing through tall grass below the paved parking lot.

One of the elderly residents smiled and waved from an apartment window, watching them cross through the tall grass. Ailyn and Connie both naturally returned the greeting as they entered the deeper woods out of sight.

"Let's find a safe place to stop," Ailyn whispered. "How about over there by that culvert?"

Sitting down on two large smooth rocks felt awkward. Neither of them could relax. Ailyn opened her get-home bag. Dan had assembled it for basic emergencies. She took inventory and emptied the contents of her carry bag into the camouflaged black/green knapsack, assuring Connie that they both would be okay. She took out a small pink-handled, snub-nosed revolver with a holster and concealed it under her windbreaker.

Connie smiled and said. "Oh, that's cute; how long have you been packing heat, woman?" They shared a nervous chuckle, and it felt good. Laughter gave them both hope.

"It's a long way to your house. Let's see what you have in your bag."

All nonessentials were wrapped inside a plastic grocery bag and stored in the extra carry bag. Ailyn began to stash it alongside the trench in case they could retrieve it at a later time. A twig snapped, and a young soldier stood above her.

"Don't be afraid. I'm not going to hurt you."

The women froze; fear stopped them from running.

"What do you want?" Ailyn asked with her concealed hand on the pistol.

"I saw you go into the woods behind the parking lot." The soldier was young as if he were just out of high school. "I'm from Onalaska. My parents and my sister are alone at home. I need to help them, so I followed you. I guess I'm going AWOL."

"We're walking to her house," Ailyn stated.

"Do you want to come with us?" Connie asked, and Ailyn glared at her.

"I would like that if it's okay."

"What's your name?" Ailyn asked.

"Private Callahan, Ma'am," he said back.

"No, your first name?" She smiled.

Somewhat embarrassed, he answered back, "Peter."

"My name is Ailyn, and this is Connie. Do you know what happened, Peter? Why are the soldiers here?"

"Well, do you know about President Pruett?"

"Yes, we heard this morning before the internet went down. Is he alive?"

"My lieutenant was talking to someone on the satellite phone; he was told that the President didn't make it." Peter looked down as he spoke of the loss.

"The whole country is under martial law, and our platoon convoyed from Fort McCoy to secure the hospitals and the freeway bridge over the River." Peter started to shake his head from side to side.

"Our orders were to use whatever force necessary. I'm sorry, but I didn't sign up to hurt Americans. I need to help my family get out of the city before it's too late."

"The whole country is without power, then?" Ailyn asked. "Who did this?"

"We were only told what happened. They didn't tell us who was responsible."

"Okay, we can stay together, but you might want to get rid of your uniform," Ailyn suggested. He changed out of his Army Combat Uniform, but his gray t-shirt over his OCP pants and black boots still screamed 'soldier'. Still, it was better than the solid operational camouflage pattern.

They placed his belongings in another plastic grocery bag and stashed his rifle above the culvert opening. It was too difficult to conceal.

****

Ailyn saw the freeway bridge just ahead. Stranded vehicles lie abandoned in disarray. The damage inflicted by the military plow trucks was evident. People walked west toward the city, perhaps wishing for salvation, answers, or care.

"How do we get past all the people?" Connie asked.

"We'll walk right up there with everyone and then slip off to the other side." Ailyn's confidence was contagious.

The terrain became more difficult as they traversed through heavy brush and thick thorn patches. Ailyn found a deer path that took them the rest of the way up the hill. She thought about the open La Crosse landfill fields. They would need to go around the fence, over Hwy 16, and the horseshoe ridge. A steady sound of gunfire echoed in the distance, coming from the north side of La Crosse. Ailyn shared her plan.

"Let's try to get to your house before dark, Connie."

"What if we follow the back roads to get over to Hwy 53?" Peter suggested. It would put them in the open, but they would make better time. The woods and the hills were challenging. They all agreed on the easier route. Only one thing mattered: getting home and reuniting with their families.

Semi Load of Donuts

Day 1, 4:23 p.m.

Melrose, WI

Ace and Greg rode their dirt bikes along the off-road trail. High grass and an occasional fallen tree or branch made steady riding a challenge.

People were becoming more unpredictable as the day went on. Ace couldn't anticipate what danger lay ahead. Look what he had already experienced: stealing two bikes and using his pistol. Not an ordinary day's work in the concrete business.

Riding to the bridge crossing on Hwy 108 was still the best option to get over the Black River. His bike started to spit and sputter. Reaching down to the fuel petcock, he turned it over to reserve and motioned to Greg that he needed to fill the near-empty gas tank. They stopped the bikes on a long straightaway; Ace unstrapped his red plastic gas can, refilling his bike first, and the rest went into Greg's tank.

"We should be able to make it to Ettrick before running out again," Ace told Greg.

****

Surrounded by trees on both sides of the trail, they eventually came up on a small group assembled at a road crossing. Some of the men appeared to be armed. One motioned for them to stop.

They slowed down as if they were going to stop and talk. Ace could see a clear path to the other side of the road. He nodded to Greg, and they both put their hands on the throttles, and power shifted past them into safety. Both men had agreed earlier to avoid people. This strategy has worked so far. Close to an upcoming intersection, Ace motioned to Greg to stop; he wanted to see if anyone had followed them, or if they could detect any signs of a trap

****

Except for some abandoned vehicles along the bridge deck, the bridge across the river appeared clear. Greg rode up next to Ace and yelled.

"If we can make it around Melrose, maybe we can take Highway D to Ettrick; otherwise, we're not going to make it before dark."

They turned left onto Highway 54 and drove past a BP gas station. Two middle-aged couples stood outside on the sidewalk, watching them as they shifted to highway speed.

Riding the open backroad put Ace deep into thought. He wondered how bad things had gotten. He thought about President Pruett. *Was he still alive*? He wondered about his friend Bill Diller who had a Ham radio; that would be useful right now.

Who took out the power grid? *North Korea*? They never accepted the restrictions former President Mrung laid on them. It was just a matter of time before they went back on their word; after all, when you're in the rat race, the only one to win the race is the lead rat.

Greg yelled, bringing him back to the present.

"We've got company, Ace!" he said, pointing at a large pack of off-road bikes and ATVs catching up behind them. They couldn't outrun them; it would have been suicidal. They pulled over and shut off their bikes as the group surrounded them; Ace's ears continued to buzz even when the motors went silent.

A voice called out. "Greg, is that you?"

"Who's asking?" Greg spoke back, the evening sun shining straight into his eyes and face.

A mature man dismounted an older red four-wheeler. He instructed everyone to lower their weapons.

Ace assumed this man was the respected leader of this organized group.

"Greg, its Ben Coulter. You guys poured the concrete for my calf barn last year."

Greg sighed with relief.

"Hi Ben, am I glad to see you! We got stuck in traffic coming out of the plant this morning. We're trying to get back to Ettrick."

"Any news on what's going on out there?" Ace asked.

Ben replied, "Last we heard, the President got hit by some crazy suicide bomber. We think North Korea or China dropped some kind of smart bomb on us. Been off the grid ever since. Everything- electricity, internet, and phones are all knocked out, but there's still a lot of chatter on the CBs."

"Is anybody in charge, or is the country on its own?" Greg asked.

"Well, we don't know, but I guess I'm in charge right now." Ben looked around at his men for affirmation.

"Can you guys help us get to Ettrick before dark, Ben?" Greg asked.

"Too risky, but I promise you'll have full bellies tonight, and we'll see what we can do to help you in the morning."

Ace had trouble accepting the delay, wishing they had taken an alternate route. It could be for the best. The dirt bikes didn't have headlights.

Joining in with the pack of riders, they drove to Ben's farm. The sun was almost down, hidden by an overcast sky.

They turned down a long gravel driveway and stopped in a barnyard. A colossal bonfire lit up the night sky. The scene was surreal; it reminded Ace of the movie 'Red Dawn.'

Ace thought again of Ailyn and the kids. He felt homesick, knowing they were on their own and probably scared.

The valley was secluded, surrounded by ridge tops and woods. Several men were preparing food on open grills cut from metal fifty-five-gallon drums.

They shared plates of grilled meat and campfire-baked potatoes with Ace and Greg. Ace was surprised at how hungry he was, but they had only eaten a small amount of food from his lunch box.

"Hey Ben, thank you for helping us," Greg called out from across the commotion of the fire.

"No problem, Greg. You guys look exhausted. When you're ready, find a place down on the straw in the calf barn, okay? I've got some things to take care of in the house. I'll see you in the morning." Ben walked to the back door of his house and went inside.

The two men walked together to the barn. "Must be some kind of militia group," Ace whispered.

"Yeah, back in 2020, I heard something about it. I didn't know it was Ben, though."

Ace was exhausted from the day's events. His thoughts were of his family. He was confident that he had prepared them for a day like this; it felt imminent. In a few short minutes, he was fast asleep.

****

Ace woke early, the sunrise creeping up over the eastern horizon line. He saw piles of unorganized firewood, cars, trucks, tractors, and even some big rigs with trailers. He had fallen asleep to the steady hum of the auxiliary power units last night. One of the men had parked a refrigerated semi-trailer between the house and the calf barn. The timing must have been on the driver's side; being near the farm before the roads jammed, allowed it to be driven down the narrow backroads.

Ace noted the group's preparations; they were true survivalists! It was fortunate that Greg knew them, or it could have turned out badly. These men thought through all the details. He thought about how most people lived, day to day or week to week, with no thought of what catastrophe could be around the corner.

Where were all the women and young children? Not a single female in sight. This unanswered question gave Ace pause; he felt uneasy, deciding not to ask, assuming they were all safely hidden away at another location. This decision would undoubtedly be reasonable under the circumstances.

Ace wanted to get on the road as soon as possible. He was concerned about Ailyn, sensing that she was in danger.

"Greg, can we get going soon?"

"Yeah, I'm almost ready."

Ace had his pack on and was ready to leave. Ben and a few of his men sat together on the old, painted wooden porch steps.

"Good morning," Greg said, offering up the first greeting.

"Morning, how did you sleep?" Ben asked. "I suppose you're anxious to get home to your wives?"

Ace felt uncomfortable answering. Greg piped right in, though. "I'm sure Cathy's worried sick. I'll feel better knowing she's okay."

"Well, you should be home in less than an hour, but please, have a couple of donuts before you go!" Ben said, passing him a full aluminum cake pan.

"That Trip Quick truck is full of bakery items. We need to eat a couple of pallets of donuts before they go stale." The men all snickered—more than likely having already consumed their fill of the high-calorie confections.

"Ace and I appreciate you and your men helping us, Ben," Greg stated again before taking a giant bite from his maple-frosted long john.

"You guys seem pretty handy. You sure I can't convince you to just stay with us?" Ben asked. "Always room for two more!"

Greg took a breath between bites, but Ace cut him off.

"If we get squared away at our places, maybe we will make it back this way again."

Ben ordered. "You four, get them to Ettrick and then come back on the snowmobile trail. I want you to stop by the Goodman farm and check in on old Earl, make sure he's comfortable, okay?"

The two men shook Ben's hand and headed to their stolen

dirt bikes.

"Take care of yourself, Greg," Ben said. "Come back if you need to."

"Thanks, Ben."

The six machines sounded loud on the peaceful farmland as they took off down the long gravel driveway and onto the rural backroad. Greg and Ace had to push their small bikes to capacity to keep up with their young escorts.

Ace saw movement on the other side of the wooded fence row; a young woman and a small girl holding wicker baskets stopped at the edge of the alfalfa field, watching the riders pass. After seeing them, Ace's trust in the group changed.

The pack of riders slowed down and turned back onto Highway D again, ignoring the stop sign. Laws no longer held the same priority, a drastic change in less than 24 hours. Soon they had made it to a familiar intersection nicknamed Four Corners.

A popular little bar called the 'Happy Hollow' stood alone, tucked into the hill side of the southeast corner. The neon signs were unlit, but the owner had propped the door open with a broken cinder block.

A few locals sat inside at the bar. They couldn't resist the escape from reality. Their job was to help the owner consume perishable inventory before it spoils. And, maybe they'd just given up hope—one last binge before facing their new lives.

The bar stood guard over the South Beaver Creek Bottoms, a public hunting ground Ace had spent much time in.

He once owned twenty acres up the road from the Hollow. When they first bought the land, he had plans to build an underground bunker there to escape in an emergency. Instead, they sold the property to help finance their new home in Galesville.

It was rare for him to patronize the rural tavern. As a recovered alcoholic, he did not need to be there. Bittersweet memories of campfires and summer recovery celebrations came to mind.

****

Abandoned vehicles blocked the North Beaver Creek bridge that crossed into the town of Ettrick; luckily, the bikes fit between and could cross.

The security escort wasted no time turning around and making tracks back to their home base—Ace and Greg nodded in gratitude and thanks to the four men.

Greg led Ace through town to his house. They turned into the driveway, stopped in front of the garage, and shut off the bikes.

Greg's wife came running out of the back door and saw it was her husband. She ran to him, grabbed hold, and kissed his face.

"Oh my God, Greg, you're home! I didn't know if I was going to see you again."

She held back no emotions, and he consoled her. "We made it back, honey. I'm here."

Ace smiled at their reunion but was eager to have his own, and his thoughts returned to getting home.

"Greg, it's been a hell of a few days; I'm going to keep going."

"Oh shit! Cathy, this is Ace. I wouldn't have made it back without him."

"Thank you so much, Ace. It's nice to meet you. Are you hungry? Can I fix you something to eat before you go?"

"Thank you, but I need to get back to Galesville. I hope my wife is home when I get there. She was working in Onalaska when the power went down."

Greg shook Ace's hand.

"Thanks again, Ace. I hope this isn't the last time we see each other." The handshake turned into a quick man hug.

Ace grabbed hold of the handlebars of his bike and raised the kickstand. Leaning the bike against his side, he backed it up to face the road and got on. One kick and it fired up again; his get-home bag replaced the empty red gas can behind him on the seat. He waved and started up the concrete driveway. The town road that led to State Highway 53 was clear of traffic, but the gas station on the edge of town was busy with vehicles and people. It appeared most of them were hoard buying. They were unprepared and trying now to supply themselves.

Ace dipped down into the ditch and sped past them. His dirt bike had no speedometer. He felt like he was easily going twenty-five miles an hour over the legal speed limit and shifted into fifth gear.

The song 'I Can't Drive Fifty-five' popped into his mind as he hit full throttle; the rest of his drive was being fueled solely by testosterone.

The Lister's

Day 1, 6:37 p.m.

Onalaska, WI

Walking the side roads made bypassing the interstates and traffic congestion possible. Hiking over the ridges through dense terrain would have been extremely difficult. Ailyn and Connie were happy that Peter suggested the easier route, but it still took them all day to make the journey by foot. They paused many times to avoid larger groups of people.

The Village of Holmen's expanding population prompted a new medical facility. Cryo Healthcare built a new complex in 2024 behind the Bernards box store. Bright lights illuminated the skyline as a beacon, drawing in the lost like bugs to a zapper.

People scurried around in the south side parking lot. Indeed, many suffered from mental fatigue, exhaustion, and stress from the day's events. The strong military presence in the building controlled them.

The group kept going on the highway, weaving between scattered vehicles. The military convoy used the same strategy here: a path of destruction, opening the center lane, veering down the off-ramp, and taking command of the hospital complex by force.

Peter explained the strategy.

"Securing the medical facilities was our primary objective, no matter the cost. Your hospital was the first target, then this one, and then the downtown La Crosse hospitals."

Ailyn reiterated. "So, you said all the soldiers we saw this morning are only securing the hospitals and the I-90 bridge, right?" Peter nodded. People fled in that direction and headed toward the new hospital's sanctuary. While walking, they heard constant gunfire and explosions throughout the day. No one could imagine what or who was shooting this much and why. It sounded like a war movie, foreign to Midwesterners' ears.

"Let's keep avoiding people. Maybe we can cross the freeway fence over by the crane company to get to your place, Connie." Ailyn was committed to staying away from the groups of panicked people.

"I'm almost home. Thank you for letting me come with you." Peter's house was just past the Legion Hall on Twelfth Street. He would need to walk down the on-ramp.

"Good luck Peter." Connie placed a hand on his shoulder.

"Everything's going to be okay." Ailyn's optimism gave Peter a new determination.

"Take care of yourselves. Thanks again." Ailyn and Connie watched as Peter hurried down the ramp and out of view.

Ailyn assured her friend. "Won't be long now, Connie; we should be at your house in less than half an hour."

"Hey lady, what's in the bag?" Ailyn's hair stood up on the back of her neck, sensing how near the stranger's voice was behind her. She ignored the question until feeling a strong tug on her get-home-bag.

Connie clenched her fist, pivoted, and put all 5'11" arm's length into the stranger's face, knocking him to the ground.

The man scrambled back and hid behind a small car, confused about what had just hit him.

Ailyn and Connie ran from the would-be assailant.

"Are you ok, Ailyn?" Connie asked.

"You leveled that guy."

They giggled as they moved along the freeway fence, relieved that they were safe and nothing worse had happened. Connie shook her right hand, feeling pain in her knuckles.

Getting to the other side of the six-foot-high steel fence was the most demanding physical challenge of the day. The surrounding trees were tall enough to climb, allowing them to jump down on the other side.

"Oh my God, I hope everyone is okay!" Connie's garage door was closed; the secret code for the neighborhood that 'The Listers' were not accepting company.

"Hello! Chris, are you here?" Connie cried out as she unlocked and opened the door and ran inside. Ailyn closed the door behind them.

"Connie, is that you?" Chris called up from the basement. Her two children screamed and jumped up and down, excited and crying, happy to see their mother.

Connie ran downstairs, meeting them at the bottom of the steps. Six-year-old Dannika stood frozen, unable to speak. Connie picked her up and held her tight, then kissed her all over her face.

Three years older, Anthony wrapped his arms around his mother's waist and held onto her. The family became one and held each other.

Chris glanced up the steps as Ailyn stood on top of the landing.

"Are you okay, Ailyn? Come on down!" She joined them and got pulled into the emotional group hug.

"We weren't sure what to do, Connie. I couldn't call you on my cell. We stayed here hoping you'd make it home soon." Chris asked. "How did you do it anyway? Oh my God, look at you; you're all scratched up. Kids, grab Mommy and Ailyn some water from the cooler. Tell me what happened?"

"It's okay, Chris, I'm home; that's all that matters."

Connie held out the water bottle; Ailyn grabbed it and chugged it down without breathing.

They heard shots outside and jumped to attention. The kids screeched and grabbed their Mom. She held and consoled them; they had been through so much in such a short time. Everything felt unfamiliar; she was relieved to be home.

"Ailyn, please stay with us tonight," Connie said.

“Traveling home alone at night is too dangerous.” It was a ‘tell’, not an ask. She and Ailyn felt the danger and knew the violence outside would intensify.

“She's right. Let’s fix something to eat and try to get some rest. Is the door locked upstairs?” Chris asked, concerned about security.

Ailyn saw Connie look over at her as she was the last one through the door. “I don’t think so.” She replied as Chris was making his way back up the basement steps. She didn’t think to turn the lock when they came in.

At the top of the landing, Chris met a strange man in his living room, holding a piece of galvanized pipe from his right hand. With the noise of the reunion in the basement, they hadn’t heard him come in.

“What the hell?” Chris barely got out the last word as the man swung the pipe and struck his forehead.

Connie screamed after seeing Chris fall at the top of the stairs.

“Hey bitch, remember me?” It was the guy Connie punched; he had followed them here.

Connie pushed her children through the open bathroom door.

Ailyn stood at the side of the staircase. She recognized the voice. He started down the wooden stairs. Again, Ailyn’s hair stood up on the back of her neck.

She pulled out the Smith and Wesson she had from her waistband and then, just like when Ace had her practice, cocked back the hammer. As the man came downstairs, Ailyn could see his profile; pipe raised in his hand, he had a rough un-shaven look and a visible red mark on his cheek where Connie had punched him. His black-framed glasses tilted off-center on his face with hair combed by dirty fingers. Ailyn aimed and fired. The bullet passed straight through his neck, spraying blood everywhere. The stranger’s stunned expression fixed on her as he collapsed onto the concrete below. His limp body hit the floor with a loud thud.

The steel pipe bounced, then rolled and stopped at the edge of the finished wall.

Connie screamed and heard her children crying behind the bathroom door.

Ailyn's ears rang. The gunshot temporarily deafened her; when at the range, she always had proper ear protection. Connie tried to shelter Dannika and Anthony from seeing the dead man's corpse, a blood pool oozing around his head. She tried to calm them down, but it wasn't working.

Ailyn moved toward the man, still aiming. She was confused, she had shot without warning. It was out of character. She believed she was a fair, kind, and gentle person. Standing there, she was fixated on the pool of blood slowly flowing to the painted floor drain.

Both women looked up, hearing Chris stir at the top of the stairs. He let out a low groan. Connie was relieved to see him. She was overwhelmed with what to do next- kids in the bathroom crying, an injured husband, a dead man on her basement floor, and her dear friend holding a fired gun, looking shocked. It was all overwhelming. Chris looked down the steps and took in the scene below. It was a lot to absorb as he regained consciousness.

"Ailyn, are you okay?" he asked.

She looked up at him, flooded with emotions- fear, relief, shock, disgust, and pride. She started shaking and crying and gently put the gun down. Killing a person was an unnatural experience. She grew up on a farm; she didn't even like butchering chickens, but it was a part of her family's tradition. When she hunted with her husband, seeing an animal dying was too much for her to handle.

Ailyn was a mother, a best friend, a wife, and a nurturer. She knew logically she would act again if placed in a similar circumstance. Chris wiped his forehead with the bottom of his shirt. He made his way down the stairs slowly, using the handrail for balance and trying to shake off the pain and the ringing in his ears.

Looking at the motionless mass lying in a heap beneath him, Chris grabbed an old blanket and covered the body, not out of respect for the dead but to shield everyone from the ongoing horror.

Connie embraced her husband, relieved to be home with him and yet distraught from the extraordinary events that had happened since she and Ailyn arrived about 45 minutes ago.

Chris opened the bathroom door and knelt to the kids, an arm around each of them, and said, "Kids, Ailyn saved us from an evil man; he can't hurt you or Mommy, but let's not look at him, okay? I want you to come upstairs with me, come on, come with me."

Anthony looked over his father's shoulder at the bloodstained blanket. He just couldn't help it.

Chris completed his original task and locked the front door.

Connie grabbed hold of Ailyn and held her. She knew her friend was agonizing over the man she had just killed.

"I didn't lock the door, Connie. I didn't lock the door." Ailyn looked up at her with a mix of panic, fear, and regret.

Both women felt a whirlwind of emotions. They were two best friends who had been through more in one day than most people ever have to endure.

"It's not your fault Ailyn; don't blame yourself." Connie tried to reassure her; facing her and holding both hands, she said, "With everything we've been through, the last thing on your mind was to lock that stupid door. Thank you for saving us! You're my hero Ailyn; you know that?"

They helped each other up the stairs leaving the basement mess behind them.

The kitchen drapes were nearly closed. A single solar light beamed on the patio deck through the narrow opening.

Chris swept the locks again, ensuring the house was as secure as possible.

"Mommy, I had an accident. Can you help me, please?" Said a sad and ashamed little girl, a natural response for a child experiencing trauma and fear.

"Oh honey, no problem. Let's get you cleaned up and get some dry pajamas on, okay!" Connie walked Dannika into the bedroom.

Chris spoke up, seeing that Ailyn was in a state of shock.

"Are you okay, Ailyn? Can I get you anything?"

She sat blank-faced, staring toward the refrigerator. It looked like she was focusing on the children's pictures and conjuring up justification for what she had just done.

Thou shall not kill, was instilled deeply in her mind from her strict Catholic upbringing. She violated the sin that seemed the easiest to obey. She felt the tug of war between right and wrong, good and evil, plaguing her soul. "I wish Dan was here," she blurted out, deeply missing her other half and feeling so alone in her grief. "He would know what to do next. I'm so sorry, Chris." She broke down in tears again. Connie and a dry, relieved Dannika were coming back down the hallway.

Chris, assessed the room. His children needed him; they needed a positive distraction.

"C'mon, you guys, let's go to the pantry and see if we can find something to make for a snack before bed, okay?" He mused silently, what does one serve two grade school-aged traumatized children as a snack with a dead man in the basement?

Ailyn and Connie were exhausted, physically and emotionally spent, from the journey home. Neither could think of food. And everything that had happened in the last hour.

They made their way down the hall toward the bedrooms. Connie went into hostess mode.

"Let's grab the kid's mattresses and put them in our bedroom. We can all sleep in the same room tonight. Anthony and Dannika can sleep on the full, and you can have Dannika's single."

The unfamiliar surroundings, and noises of the night,

made for a restless night. Ailyn dozed on and off. She kept waking up throughout a reoccurring motion picture of memories. The thought of the dead man's body and soul lying beneath her in the basement haunted her dreams. Is this man's spirit still rising? Or is it falling into the next existence? It took hours for her exhaustion to overcome her mind; she fell into a dreamless sleep after tossing and turning for hours.

****

A habitual early riser, Ailyn made her way down the hall to the kitchen, feeling the effects of an empty stomach. Connie followed her out, closing the door behind her, allowing the kids more time to sleep.

Chris was already up preparing breakfast without the convenience of electricity.

"Fresh fruit, bread, cereal, what would you like, Ailyn?" Chris asked. Despite the dead body lying in his basement, he sounded pretty chipper.

"Thanks, Chris; I'll have some fruit, please."

"Is there anything else you need, Ailyn?"

"I wish I could brush my teeth. Do you have an extra toothbrush?"

"I think we do; I'll go find you one."

Chris went to the basement steps and stopped at the sight of the blood-stained blanket. He was on a mission of service. He made his way downstairs to the basement bathroom without hesitation and re-emerged.

"A brand new one, just for you!"

"What time is it?" Connie asked.

Everyone might look at their cell phone on a typical day, but Ailyn glanced at her wristwatch and said aloud. "Six-sixteen."

"It feels like when I go to work in the morning," Connie broke down again. Chris went to her side and held her. Ailyn wasn't thinking of routine or work.

“I think we should bike the trail to Trempealeau and then take the country roads to my house. Dan will have a plan on how we can get through this.”

“Ailyn,” Chris paused for a second, then continued. “We decided last night to stay here in our house. Help is going to come. The government will straighten this out, and things will return to normal. We just have to give it some time.”

“No way, you all have to come with me.” Ailyn was surprised by their optimism that things would so easily pass.

“How do you know Dan will be there?” Connie gently asked, realizing how difficult it must have been to hear those words at that moment.

“I just know that’s all. Dan told me to meet him at the house, and that’s where he’ll be. We’ve always made our emergency plans, and that has always been our plan,” she said with conviction and faith.

“We can’t go with you, Ailyn. I’m sorry. I understand; I’m so happy and grateful to be home. Thank you for helping me. We’re going to stay, though, okay?” Connie put her hand on Ailyn’s shoulder.

Both children came running in and embraced their parents, happy to have them both home. Ailyn knew it was time to get started on her trip.

“Can I use one of your bikes, Connie?”

“Probably have to adjust the seat a little,” Connie replied

“Oh, ya think,” Ailyn stated back, playing along with her humor. Ailyn was at least six inches shorter than her friend.

With her get-home emergency bag restocked, revolver reloaded and concealed under her jacket, she hugged her friend and said quick goodbyes to Chris and the kids.

She pedaled down the concrete driveway and out onto the street. Ailyn looked back and waved, experiencing a strong feeling that it might be the last time she would see her dear friend.

****

Out on the main roads, people moved about with intention. They collected belongings, strapped things onto carts, or placed them in wheelbarrows and shopping carts. One family pulled a toboggan hooked onto a bicycle with a piano dolly on the back loaded with picture frames, a small metal safe, and different-sized plastic totes; it didn't steer well, strapped down with bungee cords and ropes. The high-traffic roads were all jammed. Nobody was going anywhere unless on foot or, like Ailyn, on a bicycle.

She didn't hear many gunshots, but the southeastern winds carried the smell of gunpowder and other burnt things. Ailyn tasted the smoke in her mouth. It was peculiar that no one was walking to the bike trail. Ailyn rode forward and tried to keep her distance from the masses. Some people tried to talk to her, but she avoided eye contact.

Dumb asses, she thought. Dan was right; people are like cows and sheep following each other instead of using common sense. Making it home to her husband and verifying that her children were okay was her primary thought and that kept her pedaling even though she was bone-weary.

D.C Is Rogue

(August 10, 2026, 3:33a.m.)

Pierre, SD

After meeting with the Governor of South Dakota for a night of fundraising and brushing elbows, Vice President Baylor woke up early. It wasn't unusual for him to start his day with only three hours of sleep. He glanced at the room's alarm clock, 3:33, shaking his head and wishing for at least another few hours of well-deserved sleep.

He opened his hotel room door. "Good morning, Sir, can't sleep?" asked his secret service detail stationed in the hallway.

"Good morning, McNally. No, like usual, my insomnia has kicked in. I'd like to return to D.C. and sleep in my bed. Can we bump up our departure time and leave earlier this morning?"

"Sure thing, Sir, I'll make the arrangements; plan on a Zero Five Hundred hours departure time, Sir."

"Thank you, McNally; I'll be ready to leave the room when you call."

Marine Two lifted off the pad at exactly Zero Five Hundred Hours and had an expected ETA of approximately Zero One Hundred Three Nine Hours in Washington, D.C.

The crew received an emergency radio transmission causing the flight to divert immediately to Norad Mountain Sanctuary in Idaho at Zero Seven Hundred Oh Three, landing at Zero Nine Hundred Three Six.

****

Inside the mountain sanctuary, thousands of feet below sea level a minority of earth's former inhabitants—the privileged ones endowed with experience, responsibility, and power- now included the Vice President of the United States of America.

The situation room was like a beehive. Everyone was on

task, working on the country's behalf.

Vice President Baylor was no longer subject to his superior's command. President Pruett had passed. A bomb fragment lodged deep into his heart, and he couldn't be saved even with current medical technology. The President's surgeon attempted and failed to perform transplant surgery.

Hearing the news shook the Vice President. He held back his emotions. It took all he had to muster strength instead of weakness.

He came from solid stock; Baylor men were soldiers, officers, and trusted public servants. Most entered into politics, a civic duty bred into their nature.

The Baylor family learned to withstand the constant barrage of negative press and criticism. Some of his ancestors may have had it easier; the court of popular opinion swayed and leaned many directions over time.

The current media suggested the current administration took a hard line that didn't benefit the majority. Trust was a commodity in modern politics, often driven by contributions and influence. Greed and power became a byproduct of the actual catalyst, the almighty dollar.

Much of this was orchestrated by the informal leaders, those that hide from the public eye. The real power lies with the establishment that could orchestrate and implement a U.S. ending strategy.

In Baylor's eyes, opposition party members like Regina Putman manipulated public opinion with the mantra of 'no one wins if we can't have it our way.' It was a dangerous political strategy as it countered the checks and balances of democratic power and diplomacy.

When he entered the conference room, all Cabinet members, primarily military, surrounded the table and stood out of respect. He was walking into his inauguration. In just minutes, he would become the new Commander in Chief.

"Let's make this formal, Sir," said Secretary of State Bailey Saxton.

“Sir, please raise your right hand and repeat after me.”

The whole ordeal felt surreal. “I will,” the new President said solemnly. He was aware that his body reacted to this with perspiration. Even a president wasn’t immune from these reactions.

Once the swearing-in was complete, the room changed from formal to business.

“Somebody bring me up to speed. Who’s responsible for this mess?”

“Mr. President, somehow Middle Eastern terrorists working inside the government disrupted the power grid using Space Force, no power,” said General Palmer. “D.C. has gone rogue. We’ve tried to enact martial law, but the whole city turned to chaos an hour after the power went down and the bombs exploded. The Capital is gone, Sir, along with the White House. The remaining citizens have no assistance from the military or the government.”

“Our East Coast military bases were all hit simultaneously, along with almost all of the Space Force satellites. We’ve reestablished drone communications linked to the one orbiting satellite that sustained no damage during the strike. Its trajectory orbit has purposely been changed to prevent any damage from the debris field, and a perimeter firmament bubble is now established around it.”

“Are any of our ground forces still intact and mobilized?”

“Yes, Sir, draw a straight line south from Michigan; all of our bases west of that line are intact and awaiting orders for deployment, Sir.”

“Oh my God.... okay; do we know of any other damage?” President Baylor swallowed a shallow dry breath, then pointed to the pitcher of water near the center of the conference table. A glass of water appeared in front of him.

“No, Sir, I’m sorry. The country is under a nationwide martial law order, as you requested. All existing National Guard troops have been activated and are currently proceeding with Plan 1-Alpha.

"I'll leave the military strategies up to you to coordinate. We need to protect our borders and assist all vulnerable remaining citizens. Is there evidence that any enemy forces are moving in on us yet?"

"No breach over the demarcation lines, but we have noticed all the nuclear-capable countries went to red alert after establishing Def-con 1. Tensions are high, and communication is limited."

President Baylor paused to drink from his water glass. "Okay, make every possible effort to inform our adversaries that we pose no threat. We don't want anyone to start punching in launch codes."

Fifty Push-Ups

(August 10, 2026, 3:33a.m.)

Minneapolis, MN

Why am I up so early, Karla thought, looking up at the ceiling and thinking it odd that it was precisely three-thirty-three in the morning. Unable to fall back asleep, she got up and put on her workout clothes, and left for an early morning run.

****

When she got back, she got ready and left for work; she loved her work and always enjoyed the sound of the river rushing past the stone retaining wall behind the museum.

Her key turned the steel door knob that pulled outward from the building.

"Morning, Scott. Is everything ready to open?"

"Hi Karla, yeah, everything's ready."

The ceiling lights began to flicker and then went dark. "What the heck?" Karla reached the lobby's welcome desk and picked up the phone receiver—dead silence.

Looking out the large bank of windows facing the street at the front of the museum, cars and trucks stopped in the middle of the road as traffic lights failed without warning. Sirens and horns began to fill the air. Drivers and passengers stopped and stepped out of their vehicles.

"Scott, did the power just go out?"

"Hey, guys, did you hear? Someone assassinated the President in D.C." Todd, a security guard, walked out of a hidden maintenance door that led to the lower levels of the Pillsbury Flour Museum.

Scott and Karla stood with their co-worker as he shared the news, and then his phone service stopped.

"Do you think we should go home, Karla?" Scott asked.

"I don't know; maybe the electricity will come back on?" Karla thought about an electromagnetic pulse; it would have killed her phone's battery. She pulled her phone from her back pocket to a screen with no service. “I don’t have any Internet service, do you guys?”

“No, me either!”

“Uh, uh.”

“I don’t think we should open the doors until we find out what’s happening; what do you think?”

“I’m worried about Jenny and the kids, Karla.”

“Maybe you should go home.”

“I’m going to go too. I can’t leave my parents alone without power.” Todd cared for his elderly parents in a small, high-rise apartment a few blocks from the museum.

“Come with me.” Scott showed concern that Karla would be left alone in the museum.

“I’ll be alright. You guys go check on your families. I’ll be here when the power comes back on.”

Karla stood alone in the doorway, watching her coworkers walk up the sidewalk. Neither man knew of her military training. She pulled the door closed and turned the deadbolt.

From the main lobby, two staircases led upstairs to a balcony overlooking a wall of windows facing the streets of downtown Minneapolis; she could hear sirens and saw the flashing red and blue lights from an array of emergency vehicles that created a strobe effect on the surrounding buildings. She was looking at chaos.

Karla mused about the source of the power disruption. Looking outside, she caught a glimpse of something racing along the street. It was heading down the walkway toward the museum's side entrance. Six cement steps and a metal railing down the center kept the out-of-control pickup truck from ramming into the side of the vestibule entrance.

The truck hit the railing with enough force to curl it up in the shape of a parenthesis. It stabbed through the windshield, impaling the torso of the panicked driver, killing him instantly.

Karla's initial impulse was to run for the truck, but she

stayed in place as a fight broke out among the people stuck in traffic surrounding the intersection. A small group appeared outside the glass vestibule. They had moved to escape the increasing violence and the horror of seeing the bloody man inside his smashed truck.

She ran down the steps, pushed open the entrance door, and led the group to the safety of the upper balcony; they were around her age.

“My name’s Karla. I manage the museum.”

“Hi Karla, I’m Alex, and this is Bjorn and Liam.”

“I’m Peter, and this is Racheal and Gianna. It’s insane outside. Thank you for letting us in, Karla.”

They stayed hidden behind the balcony wall for the rest of the day. There was no safer place to go.

Karla’s attention stayed on the street; she felt the crowd’s tone as it shifted throughout the day. She heard gunfire and watched nearby buildings burn. The smell of smoke permeated the thick walls and glass that separated her group from the carnage.

Karla excused herself several times, inviting one or two to join her throughout the day. They collected food from the staff lunchroom, as well as some blankets and cushions.

They were all stretched to their limit; Karla spent the day observing each person’s personality and recognized who had signs of strength and cunning and who might be incapable.

She noted that Alex and Peter took the initiative throughout the day for the group's benefit. Alex recommended bringing back a steel pipe he had found in the maintenance garage. Peter grabbed two fire extinguishers and carried them back to their staging area. Karla was confident that she could trust them both to step up if unexpected danger came their way. She ascertained that she was the only person with any formal training.

Karla closed her eyes briefly, exhausted from the day’s events. During boot camp, she stayed awake for almost forty continuous hours. She vowed never to be in that situation again.

Her drill sergeant stood above her and screamed, “Pillsbury, Did I catch you with your eyes closed? Get your skinny little ass off that ground and give me fifty push-ups, you worthless little fanny-melt.”

Karla opened her eyes wide, her heart racing; catching her breath, she stood up to look over the balcony's knee wall. Nothing had changed.

Five Loaves and Two Fishes

Day 2, 2:26 a.m.

Minneapolis, MN

"Did you sleep, Karla?" Alex asked as he woke up, rubbed his eyes, and stretched out his arms like he was on an overnight camping trip.

"Not much, no."

"I'll stay up for a while and keep watch if you want to try and get some sleep."

Exhausted, Karla agreed, curled up on Alex's warmed couch cushions, and covered herself with his blanket. "Please stay alert and promise to wake me up if anything happens."

"Yeah, yeah, I will. Go to sleep."

****

Karla woke up to a loud crash and broken glass shattering all over the concrete floor. She grabbed the steel pipe and ran to the balcony wall, then bolted past the maze of bodies around her to the staircase that led down to the front entrance.

Five people climbed through a broken window, gaining access to the lobby.

Karla was ready to swing with the raised galvanized pipe in her hands. The rest of the group had caught up and stood behind her. She called out from a short distance away. "Stop! Don't move!"

"Whoa, hold on, girl. Chill baby! You got nothing to worry about with us now, you hear. Calm down before somebody gets hurt," one of the intruders said.

It was seven to five; the odds favored Karla's group.

"We ain't looking for no trouble. We were just looking for a safe place to hide."

"My name is Karla," Karla said in an attempt to de-escalate the situation. She'd hear them out.

"I'm Reggie, and this is Chantelle, Oscar, Tessa, and Janasia. As I said, we're just lookin' for a safe place to hide; shits gone totally crazy out there!"

"Do you have anything to contribute? Food, weapons, skills?" Alex asked, seeing their fat backpacks; he was willing to negotiate a truce and make an informal alliance. Karla looked his way and nodded.

Chantelle opened her backpack and handed Karla an unopened bag of red licorice.

Bjorn said, "Okay, you're in," and then laughed. Everyone joined in as the licorice bag got passed around.

"What's it like outside? Did you come from downtown?" Gianna asked the girls.

Tessa explained. "We were on our way up to Duluth when it happened. All the traffic just stopped. We locked ourselves in our van on 35 West for a while. We decided to walk this way along the river before it got light out. We didn't think anyone would be inside a museum, so we broke the window. Sorry about that!"

"Yeah, we need to find something to cover the window back up, or we'll have people trying to come in." Karla looked at Alex and Peter. Both men grabbed flashlights and headed to the maintenance garage to find a piece of scrap plywood or something to cover and secure the window opening.

"I like licorice, but we better figure out how to get more food?" Bjorn stated, not satisfied with having just candy for breakfast.

Karla agreed and shared with the group, "The museum put on a food drive for the Salvation Army last weekend. We gave everyone who donated a discounted admission. No one has picked it up yet. It's all stored in a locked storage room in the back." Karla hadn't shared this earlier, but her stomach couldn't keep it a secret any longer. Their group just increased from 7-12 and everyone was hungry.

"You're kidding me, right? Let's go get it!" Bjorn's hunger overshadowed rational thought.

"We'll need to work out a system to ration the food since we don't know how long this will last. I'm sure most of the stores have already been looted, so we don't want to run out."

Liam rubbed his belly. "You're in charge of the food, Karla! When can we eat?" he asked.

Alex and Peter returned with a sheet of half-inch plywood and some two-by-fours. Bjorn and Oscar carried a heavy table over and placed it against the sheet.

They used a cordless drill to drive construction screws into two-by-fours across the window as extra bracing. The maintenance garage was like a small hardware store.

Karla was impressed by her new associates' ingenuity. People could easily see if someone was inside the museum. All it would take was another busted glass panel, and more people could get inside. Karla needed her team to be vigilant in watching the windows.

"It will take me a little while to sort and organize the food; we'll eat in the back, and I'll let you guys know when it's ready. Rachael, can you grab that plastic tote and help me?" With the window secure, she felt better, moving onto the food.

Rachael grabbed the tote from underneath the lobby's welcome desk and dumped the contents onto the floor. Karla led her to a side door marked 'Authorized Personnel Only' and locked it behind them.

The collected foods were stacked inside a locked storage room down a short hallway, past the museum's administrative offices and the conference room.

"We'll organize it into meals, so all we have to do is fill the tote and carry it out to warm it up. What do you think?"

"That sounds smart; wow, it looks like the drive was a success! Seeing all of this food makes me hungry."

"How many people do we have?"

"Twelve"

"Like the disciples?" Rachael's comment made Karla smile.

"Exactly!" The two shared a quick moment of spiritual reflection. Each was grateful for their current safety and looked forward to eating.

"How are we going to cook?"

"Let's start with the foods we don't have to cook. We'll work through that if the electricity isn't back on by tomorrow."

"I'm glad you have your shit together, Karla. Where did you learn how to be so independent?"

"Mostly from my Dad, I guess. He's a survivalist. Come on; we're ready to go feed the masses!"

Rachael looked around. "It's a little more than five loaves and two fishes!" They both laughed and headed back to meet the others.

Five Hundred Birds

Day 2, 9:43 a.m.

Galesville, WI

Ace got off the highway and threaded over the local snowmobile trails, skirting around Galesville through farm fields and sparsely wooded areas. He stopped and hit the kill switch on the handlebars. He could see stalled vehicles blocking the road from the top of the ridge.

Under dire circumstances, the unknown is one of the hardest things to accept. Everything abruptly stopped. People will panic and act irrationally.

Emergency sirens had been blasting for two straight days. Who would turn them off? The new mayor?

The lack of resources caused a ripple effect- cars ran out of gas, electric car batteries died, and multiple-vehicle accidents halted traffic.

Inoperable streetlights jammed the intersections. Within about an hour, most metro, city, and town streets were blocked. The easiest way to travel now was with small machines, a motorcycle, or something similar, especially on the main roads. Things were quickly turning to chaos!

God, I hope Ailyn's okay, he thought, feeling unsure. *I wonder if she's home yet?*

Ace approached an intersection and crossroads in the snowmobile trail. Turning left would drop him right over the hill, down into the Bridgeview Estates subdivision. As much as he wanted to go home, he went in the other direction. He needed to check with his old friend to get some answers quickly. Bill's Ham radio was the only way Ace could find out what happened.

****

Six large fallen trees were blocking access to Bill's driveway. Ace got the impression that Bill didn't want company.

Ace hid the bike under the first tree's fallen branches. He

unstrapped his pack from the seat, swung it over his back, and traversed through the maze of unorganized fencing.

Once close enough to Bill's homestead, he called out. "Bill, it's Ace," knowing this wasn't the time to surprise his friend.

Bill's favorite gun was his semi-automatic 308 when they practiced shooting together before hunting season; Bill was a good shot. "Bill, Bill Diller, it's Ace, don't shoot!"

A voice called out from behind him. "If I wanted to shoot you, Ace, you would have been a goner at the start of the driveway."

Ace almost jumped out of his skin. "Geez, Bill, I had no idea you were there."

Bill chuckled and then coughed. "That's the way it's supposed to be."

The two friends met weekly, every Thursday night, at the Lodge in Galesville for their recovery meetings. Both men were old-timers in their sobriety, but Bill was about 20 years older than Ace.

"Glad you made it, Ace," Bill said as they walked toward the house. "Were you in your semi when the power went down?"

"Yeah, I had just made it to the plant in Black River. Now, I'm heading home to see if Ailyn is back from La Crosse. Greg Stellar and I made it to his place in Ettrick, and I thought I'd check in with you and find out what you've heard on your radio!"

"All hells broke loose; President Pruett didn't make it. They say Vice President Baylor made it to a secure facility and is trying to call the ball, but everything's down. The whole power grid is dark across the country. Nothing's flying, which is probably a good thing. At first, everyone blamed North Korea and China for the attack, but it sounds like our satellites caused the whole thing."

"What?" Ace said. This was a shock. *Internal terrorism or sabotage?*

Bill nodded. "Yeah, can you believe it? Our own Space Force weapons took down the grid. Some of my friends are worried about a foreign invasion, but nobody has made any moves yet. Now would be the time; we are down like we've never been down before."

Ace sat by the Ham radio equipment with Bill; in about thirty-five minutes, he learned enough to confirm what Bill had shared.

"So, Bill, are you ready for unwelcome visitors?" Ace asked, knowing Bill was prepared.

"Oh yeah, got a big pit dug right over there for the unfriendly ones."

Ace knew his friend was capable and would protect himself and his property. He was very glad they were on the same side.

****

Bill rested his hand on Ace's shoulder. "I'll watch for you and Ailyn if you make it back this way again."

"Thanks, Bill. I hope she's made it home."

"Well, don't let your meatloaf or your buddy hack it," Bill joked as he extended to shake Ace's hand.

Ace walked down the driveway with a new sense of urgency, confident that Bill could take care of himself through this crisis.

His thoughts were with Ailyn and the kids; he needed to know everyone was safe as the family protector. He also knew he couldn't make it through this mess alone.

He jogged back to "his" new dirt bike.

He had no idea what lay ahead. People would be unpredictable; being home-bound and without information made everyone feel helpless. Many would band together like the men he saw off of Highway D. He no longer trusted anyone's intentions.

People would hoard, food supplies would start to run out, and daily luxuries like soap and cigarettes would get scarce.

Most people would struggle without necessities like toilet paper; very few people were prepared for the worst, and most had a low threshold for such inconvenience.

It had been hard not to use his cell phone, and he wasn't a chronic 'user' like some. Imagine what they must be feeling! He understood the stress of releasing an addiction. This feeling, along with helplessness, would be hard on many. People are creatures of habit; this interruption to everyone's normal life was unprecedented. Store shelves would empty in days if not hours.

Ace also knew that even good people would perform heinous deeds to survive, protecting property and belongings. Bonds that were once the strongest broke for what you carried on your back.

Ace thought about their personal struggles and sacrifices to build Ailyn's dream home. He had finally made it to their subdivision, where it sat… now to find out if she was home.

Ace liked their neighborhood. Neighbors knew each other but kept themselves at a comfortable and respectful distance. Some had probably already bugged out, leaving to check on older parents or picking up children at college, or heading to places they felt safer. Many were probably stuck somewhere out on the roads. Looking around, he surmised the only ones still hunkered down were Mary and John, their neighbors across the street. Their camper and vehicles were still sitting at rest in their driveway.

Mary had a beautiful garden and had learned to can from her parents, just like Ailyn had. Both women had come from families that were independent and self-sustaining.

As he rode down his street, Ace tried to decide if he should check on his neighbors. Lines of cars were forming out on the highway in the distance.

People were walking, abandoning their vehicles, and making their way home to their families on foot.

Time was running out! He knew it would only be about another night, and all hell truly will break loose.

Is she home yet? "Please, Ailyn, be here waiting for me." The words came out in a whisper. He knew the shorter distance from La Crosse to Galesville would be twice as congested and much more dangerous. Her route home could take a few days.

"Ailyn, are you here?" He called out softly.

He looked around; she hadn't returned.

"Okay, get your head on straight, man," he said out loud, suddenly feeling a mix of rage and panic. Ailyn could have chosen five different routes home. He thought about looking for her but knew the odds were against him. Accepting powerlessness wasn't easy.

The basement steps were dark and would be until the backup home generator system kicked on. Noise, the dull humming sound emitted by the generator, would become a beacon for everyone within earshot. That wouldn't be good right now. Stealth movement and staying out of sight were key.

His phone flashlight wouldn't work since his phone was dead; he looked for flashlights in the junk drawer.

He lit his way down the carpeted basement steps and entered his back storage room. Two stackable storage shelves, neatly organized, held all of the survival gear he diligently collected. He grabbed a battery-powered headlamp so he could rummage and find things hands-free.

He had imagined just this exact scenario many times. Yet he still struggled to think of the first thing to pack. Reaching inside a plastic storage drawer, he picked out a folded piece of paper he had printed years ago.

Bug-out bag supplies:
Waterproof container
Birth certificate and driver's license copies
Two thermal space blankets
Two lightweight sleeping bags
Two water filtration bottles

Emergency rations
Cold weather gloves, waterproof jackets, two hats,
Two sets of natural earth-tone-colored clothes.
Six-packs of hand warmers
Two fire starters
Two headlamps
Chem sticks
First aid kit with pain-killers
Antiseptic wipes, anti-bacterial wipes, bug repellent
Compass
Multi-tool
Hatchet
Sillcock key
Duct tape
Paracord and waterproof camouflage tarp
Two hunting knives in sheaths with stash belts
Semi-auto 22 rifle, crossbow, and sling, 9mm pistol,
Ammunition
Sewing kit
Small mirror
Wrapped canned goods in towels, survival foods
Wash rags.

Out of the corner of his eye, Ace saw two dog kennels. One was Burr's, a black lab that retrieved well over five hundred birds in his thirteen-year hunting career. Burr was, beyond a doubt, the best dog Ace ever owned.

Whenever he thought about Burr, he felt the same loss and grief he experienced when he put him down two days after Christmas in 2018. The vet said. "You know you're doing the right thing, right?" And he agreed, knowing that Burr was in pain and suffering.

Burr's little buddy, Dock, a tiny Yorkshire terrier, also felt the loss. When he was only eight years old, and just three months after the loss of Burr, Dock experienced kidney failure from a tumor in his bladder. Both dogs were gone.

Losing their beloved pets felt bittersweet shortly after they moved into their new home.

Ailyn wanted to sell the crates. He thought they would get another dog someday. They hadn't, but he was relieved right now that it didn't materialize. It would be nearly impossible for him to euthanize his own pets. But, now, it would have been necessary. As much as they would have loved new companions; a dog would have made stealth travel impossible.

He carried the last of the supplies upstairs, thinking about Ailyn. He worried, wondering where she was and if she was safe. It was very hard to concentrate.

He decided to check in on their neighbors, going over and knocking on their sliding patio door. "Jeff, Bailey, are you guys' home?"

No answer. He noticed two of the three trucks missing from their driveway.

If they were home, they weren't answering their door. He went across the street to see John and Mary. While their vehicles were all in the driveway, they also didn't answer.

He wanted to help his immediate neighbors.

He imagined them huddled deep inside their basements like during the annual tornado warnings. It will even be hard to trust neighbors with such uncertainty.

The Great River Bike Trail

Day 2, 8:17 a.m.

Onalaska, WI

As an experienced cyclist, Ailyn kept an even fifteen-mile-per-hour pace. She pushed forward up the groomed pea-gravel bike path.

Strangers were her most significant concern. She knew it was 14.5 miles to Trempealeau and another six or seven by road to get home. She didn't calculate any extra time or distance for obstacles or delays.

She felt uneasy but kept moving, staying focused on her goal to get home. Dan would know what to do next.

Ailyn thought about their prior conversation about losing the power grid. She was mildly irritated that he was right; it did happen. But, also, she was relieved that they had discussed this and other disasters. He always ended his discussion by reminding her to meet him at home if anything happened.

She crossed the first bridge. As she approached the canoe/kayak launch, she heard people ahead. She decided to stop and listen more closely.

People were arguing near a group of houses southwest of the launch. While she rested and listened, she thought again that it was interesting that no one else was traveling on the bike trail. People were instead staying on the roads and adding to the congestion.

She looked down and saw dark red spots splattered on the ground. Something, or someone, had been drug across the path and towards the houses. It looked like drying blood.

The arguing became more intense and threatening. She felt her heart pound, concerned about the intensity of the noise she heard. So, she picked up her bike and tried to sneak quietly past the houses, trying to go unnoticed. The argument ended with a sudden piercing scream, gunshot, and then silence.

She froze in fear, listening but hearing nothing. Her fear

made the bike feel like a lead weight, so she lowered it back to the ground and moved cautiously up the path.

Standing at the second bridge that crossed over the downward flow of the Black River, she took a final look back at the house through the trees and brush. A man stood in the path, looking directly at her.

She froze wishing she was invisible.

He started running towards her.

A normal sixty-two-year-old would swing one leg over the bike, hit the pedal, and apply pressure to move forward. Ailyn ran forward with the bike and mounted it like a sixteen-year-old. She gained speed, out pedaling the sound of the man's breathing. She heard his footsteps on the old bridge wood planks slow down and eventually stop behind her.

Simultaneously, a loud gunshot and a whistling sound next to her left ear forced her to the right side of the path.

She didn't hear the next bullet; she felt it as it grazed her right shoulder.

A sharp burning pain and the slow ooze of red blood staining her summer jacket.

It was a minor wound but it stunned her; she wouldn't let it slow her down but it hurt like hell and would need attention once she found a safe place to stop.

She increased her speed to about twenty-one miles per hour to get a safe distance from her assailant. She couldn't maintain this pace; and slowed down to catch her breath; this encounter was unnerving.

Since they moved to Galesville, she and Dan had been on this trail many times since they moved to Galesville. A tractor path around the next corner was used by a local farmer to enter his field. It was secluded and surrounded by woods. She would stop there. Her mind wandered to happier times; they had once walked back there together, trespassing, searching for morel mushrooms and stumbled onto the rock wall foundation. They guessed the original structure had probably been built around the Great Depression, based on the amount of decay. They imagined that a young pioneering couple had perhaps tried homestead farming but failed. The world and the bank had different plans.

That day was great for Ailyn and Ace as she remembered a quick romp in the woods. Those opportunities were less frequent for the fit couple, but when they occurred, it was memorable. She smiled. It was nice to have a peaceful meaningful memory; it helped her control and reduce her heart rate from the fear, injury and getaway.

She made her way to the rock walls and hid her bike between some overgrown lilac bushes. She loved lilacs and thought again about the young hopeful homestead couple and how fragrant they must have been each spring. She sat in an inside corner of the old foundation wall which gave her space to sit and rest and open her pack.

Remnants of past visitors lay scattered around her; empty cans and bottles littered the area. No doubt other romantic encounters had occurred there. She removed the first aid kit and applied pressure to her shoulder. The bleeding slowed.

She took deep breaths and started working on her arm. She wanted to focus on moving forward and getting home. She drank almost an entire water bottle in just a few seconds. Ailyn used the rest to wet a piece of gauze to clean her blood-stained skin. It opened the clotted wound but made it easier to dress her throbbing shoulder with a dab of antiseptic cream, a bandage, and cloth tape.

The man had been arguing with a woman. After the gunshot, Ailyn didn't hear her voice. Did the man shoot and kill her in the heat of an argument? She was shaking from the terror of being chased and then shot by this stranger.

It took a second layer of tape to stick to her skin. She made sure that everything was in order and her shoulder was taken care of.

She was relieved it had stopped bleeding. Just four inches to the left and the bastard would have hit me in the head, she thought. She would have bled out on the Great River Bike Trail. She had to pace her breathing to manage the shock and fear she felt. She shuddered again.

As she thought through everything, she felt a new sense of confidence. *I should go back and put a cap in that guy's ass. I'd be doing the world a favor!*

Ailyn froze again at the sound of a twig snapping in the direction of the tractor path. Peeking over the rock wall she saw a deer slowly moving back toward her.

She and the deer watched together as the man who shot her cautiously walked down the path. He would stop and start again, looking up and back down with slow, methodical steps. *'He's tracking me,'* she thought. It was terrifying.

The deer was almost to the rock wall and had no idea a woman kneeled, frozen behind her.

When the man stepped into the woods, the doe launched sideways through the air and landed about ten feet away. In another fluid movement, barely touching the ground, it flew even further on the second bound.

Ailyn wished she could do that too. But she was prepared. She had her pistol in her hands. She stood up, aimed at the chest of the darkened silhouette, and squeezed the trigger. Time stood still and moved at lightning speed.

The shadow wracked backward against the lilacs—gurgling sounds between gasps for air. And then he stopped. Ailyn heard the silence and knew she didn't need to take a second shot.

In two days, she'd killed two men. It was too much. She leaned against the rock foundation wall, and wept. "Father God, please forgive me!" She uttered the words between sobs. In a few short moments, as if touched by His hand, she felt peace and calm. Family thoughts filled her mind. She got up, walked toward her hidden bicycle, shut the open get-home-bag, placed it over her shoulders, and pushed the bike back to the main trail. *Dan will know what to do,* she thought once more.

No one was available to evaluate her mental health; if so, a professional would have said she was in severe shock and suffering from Post-Traumatic Stress Disorder.

Only a mother's determination gave her the strength to peddle toward the home she loved and the promise of seeing her loving husband only mere miles away. She moved as if in a trance, seeing only her hands on the grips of her handlebars and the moving front tire over a solid white line along the paved asphalt.

Milkweed Plant

Day 2, 12:01 a.m.

Galesville, WI

Ace sat on the kitchen floor, his back against the lower hickory cabinets. His inner clock told him it was close to noon.

The silence was deafening.

Ailyn should be home soon, even if she's walking.

He imagined seeing her walk in from their brick patio. In his mind she would run into his arms, a reunion created by over forty years of hard work and love.

He needed to stay busy while he waited. He had already organized the secondary bug-out bags and chose weapons; all were safely waiting in the corner. His goal was to be prepared for stealth-mode travel, but could anyone be prepared? He thought about a stashed cache of extra supplies he hid at a spot along his pre-planned route. It would be a treat when they got there; it was going to be a hike and he had planted some surprises. Their goal would be to make it to Mike and Sue's within a few weeks.

When he and Ailyn designed the house, they discussed adding an underground hidden emergency shelter accessible through a Murphy door built into the poured concrete basement foundation wall. The additional expense made it cost-prohibitive, so they decided against it. Ailyn didn't know he and Mike had constructed an emergency shelter deep inside the hill behind Mike's home. Ace and Mike would make it fully operational as soon as they got there. Both men were survivalist preppers by heart, but neither had full spousal support.

Ailyn and Sue had similar views of the world, denying the possibility of catastrophic circumstances, though Sue was much more tolerant of Mike's preparedness. Both women were optimists who believed that life was somewhere between ideal state and catastrophe.

Ace was tired; he had endured thirty-two hours of minimal sleep, improper nutrition, and dehydration. Still sitting on the kitchen floor, he dozed off, dreaming of sitting in one of the two giant sugar maples in the front yard of his family's farm.

A tire attached to a large barn rope hung beneath him in the hot summer breeze. It seemed so high back then, but it wasn't—a mere ten feet or so above the ground. In his dream, he was climbing almost to the top branches, looking down on the gravel pit across the road; heavy equipment scattered and motionless on the tops of each bank. There was a run-off pond near the bottom. He saw a person floating in the water. Who was it? Someone's drowned; I need to get down from this tree. He hung tightly onto the thin maple branches. He let go of the branch, surrendering like a seed from a milkweed plant blowing in the wind and then standing at the pond's edge. It was a girl! It was his Ailyn, in her late teens, with long brown hair, dressed nicely. The girl he met so many years ago. He was wading into the pond to get her and awoke to the sound of the front door opening. He opened his eyes, and there she stood. Torn clothing, messed up hair, and scratches. She looked beyond exhausted.

"Ailyn!" He got up to hug his tired bride.

"Oh my God, I wasn't sure you'd be here, Dan," she cried. He led her to a chair. "Here, sit down, honey. Let me get you some water."

He opened a red cooler that sat on the kitchen tile. It was a gift from his employer—a high-test cooler that held its temperature for days. The refrigerator and freezers in the house were slowly defrosting. They would eat what they could before they left. He was as happy to see her as she was to be home.

"Here, it's nice and cold, Babe!" She drank until the bottle was empty and then tore into a banana and a ripened peach. Her journey had taken a toll on her. "Do you want to talk?" Ace could see the changes in her eyes. Something was different about his best friend.

In a flat tone of voice, she told him that she had killed two men. After saying it, she teared up, then composed herself, took a deep breath, and continued.

"I shot the first one at Connie's and the second one on the bike trail by that old rock foundation we found. Connie and I left Onalaska, and when we got to her house, we went in, and I forgot to lock the door behind me. A man had followed us there; we ran into him earlier. Connie hit him when he approached us earlier. When he came in, he hit Chris in the head with a pipe, and before he could get to all of us in the basement, I shot him in the neck in their basement."

"Is Chris, okay? They didn't come with you?"

"Yes; he is okay. But they wouldn't come with me, I tried to convince them that you would know what to do, but they wouldn't come. Chris thinks it's all going to go back to normal again." She took another deep breath and sighed.

"I biked the trail to Trempealeau. I heard a guy arguing with a woman near that canoe launch. As I was sneaking past, he shot her and killed her.

Before I knew it, he was chasing me! He shot at me and grazed my shoulder. I got away and made it to that old rock foundation spot. He tracked me, Dan, he tracked me, and there was this deer, and I stood up and fired. I hit him right in the chest, and he fell into the bushes. He was gasping for air, and then he was dead. I don't remember anything else until I walked in the door and saw you!"

"Holy shit Ailyn, I don't know what to say. You're such a badass!"

Maybe it wasn't the most appropriate thing at that moment. Ailyn looked up at her husband, laughing and crying at the same time.

They hugged each other as he tried to reassure her that everything was going to be okay.

"I've got everything packed and ready; we're leaving for Mike and Sue's in the morning. People will start acting crazy after three days without showers and toilets!"

"What about the kid's Dan?" Ailyn had been worried

about them since the power shut down.

"I stopped by Bill's house before coming home. I heard on his Ham radio what's happened. Hatty and Reese know where we are going. It's up to them now, Ailyn. They will come to Mike and Sue's if they want to try and get to us. They're pretty self-sufficient kids. We taught them well. They'll do whatever it takes to survive."

Ailyn's instincts weren't as cavalier as her husband's. She was worried about both of her children. Survival wasn't just about being in control. She had faced a lot to get home. She had no idea what they were experiencing. They talked for the rest of the afternoon and evening about plans and scenarios to be prepared under their new circumstances. Ailyn took a short nap to calm her frayed nerves. Day 3 would bring new circumstances.

For dinner, they ate a substantial meal together by candlelight, trying to use up foods that would go to waste without proper care.

Dan had painted the lower windows with black spray paint so no one could see in. It looked dark and empty if anyone looked in the house's direction.

"This might be our last meal in the house," Ailyn noted.

"Yeah, I thought of that too. It sucks that we might not be able to grow old here as we planned."

"Maybe everything will right itself again?"

"We can only hope," he yawned and rubbed his full belly, ready to get some well-needed rest for their long journey.

He whispered, "One last time in our Sleep Number, Babe?" They cuddled and enjoyed their time together, knowing it could be a long time before it happened again.

****

Dan and Ailyn awoke early, very comfortable and warm under the blankets of their king-size bed. Ailyn opened her eyes and saw her husband lying next to her. He was staring at the lines on her face, thinking about everything they had experienced in their time together.

"How long have you been awake?"

"Oh, about an hour, I guess. How about we just lay here forever?" Dan said, knowing it was impossible. The days to come would put them both to the ultimate test. He also knew his wife needed the rest.

They would travel by foot to ensure they stayed undetected. Stealth movement, a pace slightly faster but similar to stalking deer or turkeys, allows for the element of surprise rather than being surprised.

They needed to stay alert and prepared to maintain the upper hand in life-or-death situations. Ailyn had already experienced two incidents; they both had tested her resolve. From now on, it will be seconds at a time until they reach safety. They both had experienced violence and trauma in the first two days. So much had happened. Dan didn't want to imagine what challenges Day Three would bring. Next week or next month seemed equally impossible to imagine.

Their first stop would be Bill's. That trip would hopefully be uneventful, allowing him to teach Ailyn the pace.

"Let's try and eat a big breakfast. We have a bunch of food that's going to spoil. We're going to need lots of energy."

Dan reached over and pulled Ailyn's shirt collar down. "We should change the dressing on your shoulder before we go. I'm glad this was just a flesh wound; we need to watch it for the next few days to make sure it doesn't get infected."

"Okay," she said, nodding, then taking another bite of their last orange. She felt numb, happy to be with Ace, and happy to be home. But still numb.

"Let's head out soon." Although Dan didn't usually like it, the farmer planted corn in the field behind their house. They rarely saw any wildlife in the corn; he preferred when the farmer planted alfalfa.

The tall stalks of corn gave them the perfect cover they

needed to exit the burbs and enter the woodlands.

It was nearly two miles of steady walking to Bill's farm. Illegal trespassing, but the authorities were no longer concerned about that. They had more serious issues to attend to. Landowners could be a different story. Dan planned a route that would allow them to stay clear of any houses.

They walked past the parked dirt bike. "New bike, honey?" Ailyn pointed over at it parked on the back patio deck.

"It's a long story. I'll tell you sometime." Ace rolled it through the service entry door to the garage in case they ever got back here and needed it. He came out the door holding his folded leather cut in his hands, re-opening his pack, placing it inside, and closing it back up again.

It was difficult to get between the tight cornrows carrying all their gear, but once inside, he pushed down single stalks until they reached the fifth row.

He stopped, and Ailyn almost ran into him. She was focused on keeping up. He giggled at her a little, and she gave him that look of annoyance; she knew she should pay attention.

They stopped and took a look back at the beautiful home they were abandoning. He saw Ailyn's eyes well up with tears. He reached out a hand and gently wiped them dry.

"Remember what we talked about, honey," he said softly. She regained her focus. Their slow, methodical movements matched the sounds of corn stalks rustling in the breeze; it became a game.

Canned Peaches

Day 3, 8:04 a.m.

Galesville, WI

It only took a few hours of careful, deliberate walking: they navigated through wooded hillsides and a few more dense cornfields. Ace and Ailyn stood together on Bill's property line.

"Ailyn, if we stay at Bill's tonight and set out again in the morning, we could be on foot for over a week before making it to Mike and Sue's."

"I'm worried about the kids, Dan," she said.

"I know, Honey, but you've got to believe they're okay, and maybe, God willing, we will see them again soon. They're tough like their Momma!" he said, nudging her.

Ailyn smiled and leaned into her husband. She appreciated that he always comforted her with his subtle humor. It was one of the many things she valued the most throughout their forty-two years of marriage.

****

Soon they were back in Bill's driveway, where Ace had stood just yesterday morning.

Ailyn stood looking at the cut-off tree stumps—one, two, and three on each side. The giant oak trees must have been over one hundred fifty years old. They were planted in perfect rows, probably by Bill's great-grandfather in the late 1800s when the Diller's first settled this land. It was a shame they had to be sacrificed to accommodate the times. Their size, mass, and longevity shared the story of the nurturing and care they had received over time. Maybe this was their true reason for existence? Their logs laid horizontally across the gravel driveway, revealing their final purpose.

"Bill, it's Ace," he yelled out.

"I see you, Ace, hi Ailyn, come on up," a voice called out from the front steps.

"Hi, Bill," Ailyn smiled as they approached the weathered homestead.

Bill replied. "Ailyn, good to see you! Glad you made it

back home. Ace was concerned about you making the trip alone from La Crosse." Bill looked back at Ace, who was looking at the ground. "He and I know a few things about powerlessness. One of those situations to let go and let God handle. I'm glad you made it." Bill placed his arm around Ace's shoulder.

"Thank you for being here for us my friend. Has anyone else visited you yet?" Ace asked, knowing that if Bill said 'yes,' there might be dead bodies he would want to shelter from Ailyn.

"No, not yet, but I never get many visitors up here," Bill said, shrugging his shoulders. "I doubt if many people besides you two and maybe a few from the meetings have thought about old Bill.

"So, I can't convince you to come with us tomorrow then, can I?"

"No, I'm afraid my walking days are over. Even with these new knees, I don't think I'd make it very far; besides, you two don't need me slowing you down." He realized he hadn't asked Ace where they were going to go yet. "By the way, where are you heading anyway? Got a plan?"

"Yeah, have you met my friend Mike Sanderson? He and I have been prepping for a long time together. We'll make our way to his place just off Hwy T, past Mindoro. He and his wife have a house there that is concealed from the road, up on a hill, so we can see who or what's coming at us. Best guess, it'll take about a week to get there by foot unless we run into trouble."

"If you stay with me tonight, we can enjoy one last supper together." Silence fell over the room—a stark reminder of the unknown possibilities.

"Let's make the best of it, Bill," Ailyn spoke out first to break the silence, pulling glass jars wrapped in bath towels of canned venison, corn, green beans, and potatoes from her knapsack.

"We'll have these for dessert!" Ailyn set a glass mason

jar of canned peaches on the kitchen table.

"Oh my, not sure the last time I had a five-course meal here at the house. Your pack's going to be a lot lighter, Ailyn." Bill laughed, and it was contagious.

****

"That was delicious, honey," Ace stretched backward in his chair, trying to make room for more. "I might have to put looser pants on!"

"They'll fit better in a couple of weeks," Ailyn replied.

"Ha, no doubt." He gave her a slight smile.

"I'll clean up while you two spend some time together."

"Ailyn, Ace is a lucky man to have you."

"Yeah, not sure how she put up with me for this long, Bill," he smiled, never quite feeling that he deserved such a beautiful life partner.

"Ha, that's your alcoholism talking again, you're a great man, and she knows what she has," Bill assured his friend with a verbal pat on the back.

The couple blushed a little, sharing a glance of affection.

"Let's go into the study." The two men excused themselves; they walked through the early nineteenth-century architecture—many rooms on top of an old rock foundation basement—a typical farmstead home. Built for a large family expecting many children, but when Bill and his brother inherited the family farm, all that was left was a home full of memories and old ghosts. Everyone else was gone.

Over the years, those extra rooms were filled with antique treasures and trinkets that cost mere coins. It would be worth a small fortune if they were all auctioned off. It's sad to think that everything would become worthless if the world stays in survival mode.

The study was Bill's man cave—walls filled with dusty deer mounts and other framed trophies from his past.

He was a Vietnam War veteran. His training came from a

long, honorable life of service to his parents and country.

"Ace, I spent some time on the radio after you left yesterday. Vice President Baylor is now the President. He's underground calling the ball, probably from Norad out west. The entire country is still under martial law. Washington, DC, was the first to get hit, and then New York and it just followed from there. A group of former government officials held up somewhere in Ohio are trying to establish control again. A team of anti-government sympathizers orchestrated the attacks; they might be preparing for another invasion.

"The country has been in a state of division since 2016. How did it ever get this way, Bill?" Ace shook his head in disbelief.

"Started with The Beatles," Bill said seriously. Ace turned and looked at him, surprised. They both laughed together.

"I heard that, Bill," Ailyn called out from the kitchen. "I loved the Beatles."

****

Ace tossed and turned, unable to fall asleep. His mind raced, planning and fixing different scenarios and problems long before they happened. That was his M.O.

He anticipated so he could plan the unexpected. He didn't want to get caught with his pants down, literally or figuratively.

There was this one time, though, back in the early eighties. He and his girlfriend were in the act at his parent's farmhouse. They were on the couch in the living room when he heard the kitchen door open without a knock, and Grandma Ayer walked in on them before they could compose themselves. It was obvious, and he knew she knew.

He was so embarrassed, but she never mentioned another word, maybe thinking it was natural. She was cool that way, a naturalist with a scientific mindset.

She fit the description of a midwife of sorts. She was a

user of the ancient ways and a believer in homeopathic medicines and lifestyles. She always said she wanted to live to be 100 years old. She came so close; she did it if you counted her time in the womb. Maybe in the grand scheme of things, she believed in the theory of evolution but still hoped there was a God so she could live forever.

Ace shut his eyes and focused all his thoughts on his grandmother, finally falling into a dreamless sleep.

****

The morning came too fast. Ace opened his eyes to a nudge from Ailyn. The beautiful aroma of fried bacon and coffee awoke her. "Smells like Bill's cooking us breakfast."

Ace stretched, breathed deeply through his nose, and exhaled by mouth. "Oh my God, does that smell good!" The smell of the old wood-burning stove in the kitchen reminded him of his childhood on the farm.

It was Day Four, and he sat on the side of the bed, thinking again about the conditions and people they might encounter. Hungry, dangerous, desperate people willing to do anything to secure food, shelter, and supplies. He kept these thoughts to himself, smiling back at Ailyn.

They dressed in faded camouflage hunting clothes and went down the old wooden stairs to the kitchen.

"Good morning, Bill," Ailyn said as she entered. "That smells wonderful. Is there anything I can do to help?"

"No, young lady, this time the cooking's on me. How do you like your eggs?"

"Over easy would-be great, thank you."

"Bill, have I told you how much I appreciate your friendship?" The two men had been friends since 2017, after he and Ailyn first moved to the area.

"It's hard to find a good hunting and fishing buddy," Bill said and Ace nodded.

"Over easy good for you too?" Bill asked.

Putting a hand on his friend's shoulder, Ace nodded and

replied. “I’ve always liked sopping up the yolk with my toast!”

Time

Day 4, 10:11 a.m.

Melrose, WI

They were standing at the counter of the Sinclair gas station in Mindoro, Wisconsin when the power went down. Mike and some locals watched the news coverage of the President's assassination attempt and the bombings on T.V. until the power went out. He had no difficulty making it back home as the country roads weren't busy with traffic yet. Conversations with close neighbors over the last four days only reaffirmed his fears. He had no other way of learning what happened but planned to take every precaution. His gut told him it was not going to get better.

Mike and Sue strategically cut down some of their driveway trees, eliminating access to their ridge-top home.

"Who would have thought any of this would happen?" Sue mused, still in shock from all the change over the last four days.

"Quite a few people knew it was only a matter of time." Mike paused for a second. "Me, Ace, and Pete have had many conversations over the years. Did I ever tell you what our secret code would be if Ace and Ailyn made it up to us?"

"No, what's that?" She asked.

Mike explained, jokingly but still quite seriously, so he didn't shoot him as he approached the house; Ace would have a pair of Ailyn's panties stretched out on a stick like a surrender flag.

"So, if you see a pair of panties waving down by the tree line, don't shoot; it's probably him."

Sue laughed out loud, "Oh, Sanderson, I love you. That's pretty funny."

"If everything goes well, it should take them about a week to get here. We probably have a few others coming our way, some friendly, some not so much. We'll have to pick and choose who to trust when that time comes. Otherwise, we might have to start a cemetery behind the pole barn."

"God, I hope not," Sue shook her head from side to side. "There is strength in numbers."

"Maybe, but we've got to think about resources and safety. And, how much room we have in the bunker. Trust will be the key. I think we know who can be trusted, who'll contribute, and who will just be takers."

****

Ace looked back and saw his friend leaning against the porch pillar, watching them descend the driveway. They waved simultaneously—another stern reminder that it might be for the last time.

****

"Idaho 267647 to any current operator."

"Go ahead, Idaho 267647. Wisconsin 751976, standing by."

"Hello, this is Elan Must, calling from inside Norad Sanctuary on President Baylor's behalf. Are you a Patriot, my friend?"

"Yes, I am Mr. Must. It's a pleasure speaking with you, Sir. My name is Bill Diller. Sorry to hear the news about former President Pruett. How can I be of service?" He heard some shifting on the other side of the radio.

"Mr. Diller, this is President Baylor. First of all, I'd like to thank you in advance. Here is our current situation; we have usable radio equipment but no established network. Satellite communications are down. We need to…."

President Baylor continued to explain the plan to network the country through Ham radio communications. He asked Bill if they could piggyback his contacts to accomplish their goal of achieving real-time intelligence.

"Time is of the essence. I need to get this messaging out

to your entire network. Are you a Veteran, Bill?"

"Yes, Sir, Viet Nam, Sir."

"Well, consider yourself re-enlisted if that's alright with you?"

"Yes, Mr. President, I'm honored to serve my country again in any way, Sir!"

"Can you assure me that each of your connections will also be patriots like yourself, Bill?"

"Yes, Sir, most of them are former soldiers I served with or their surviving family members."

"Okay, thank you, Bill, and good luck with your mission. Idaho 267647 out…."

Bill thought how Ace would have enjoyed hearing that conversation.

****

Traveling by foot, Ace and Ailyn hiked quietly, knowing that regular communication could travel long distances inside wooded areas. Neither of them wanted to be seen or heard.

The two physically fit seniors methodically walked around the city they had come to love, Galesville, Wisconsin.

Ace planned the route to the west bank of the South Beaver Creek that flowed under the bridge on Ellefson Road. They could cross to the other side and hike along the power poles erected in 2018. After that, they would stay north of the Black River, following Hwy 54 East through the labyrinth of connected woods.

It was hilly terrain, but it should keep them safe and away from the local population. Strangers were the enemy until proven otherwise.

They had a few days left of summer and all of the fall to make it to their friends. It was a great time to be outside; the nights were cooler, and the mosquitos were dying down. It was a perfect time of year for foraging as well. The fertile hardwood forests were full of fresh berries, mushrooms, and other edibles.

They carried air-sealed bags of dried foods purchased from a Patriots supply company. The packets provided adequate daily calories, but they still rationed them to ensure survival.

Ace was on the lookout for a safe comfortable place to camp that evening. They were making good time, but he knew this could change as their bodies wore down from their new routine. They would feel the lack of sleep, and water, and the adjustment to different foods. Stretching their limits of suffering now would help them long-term.

Clean drinking water wasn't a concern; they used special bottles with built-in filtering capabilities. To avoid detection, they wouldn't have a fire. Enduring days without a hot meal was hard; but they had food, which was the most important thing. It placed them out of their comfort zones and would be one of the many challenges.

Killing another human being was the ultimate test, and Ailyn had already done that twice in five days. Though both were in self-defense, it couldn't have been easy. To Ace's surprise, she seemed to be putting it past her, at least in her waking consciousness. Her subconscious told a different story. Twice in the past two nights, she woke up, actively reliving the experiences that haunted her. Ace let her cry into his shoulder and held her tight, reassuring and supporting her. He knew it was better that she continues to process this now; holding back her emotions wouldn't help. They were bound to experience more trauma and discomfort, but at least now, he was with her, and she wouldn't manage it all alone.

****

Ace and Ailyn were getting used to the silence and peace of the woods. They had been traveling for a few days and were comfortable with their pace and their routines. As lifelong campers, they knew how to make and break camp.

On their second night, they woke to the sounds of off-road vehicles, which were getting louder. Headlights flickered across the dense leaf canopy resembling a disco ball. They scrambled out of their shared sleeping bag.

Both wanted to run, but they fought the urge, staying frozen instead. Trying to determine if this merry band of night stalkers was aware of their presence or just accidentally happened upon them.

"Maybe they don't know we're here, Ailyn; keep your head down, and don't look directly at their headlights," Ace remembered crossing the all-terrain trail about fifty yards behind them. If the riders had found them, it would have been like finding a lost set of keys in the dark.

The sounds of whining motors kept getting closer and closer. It was unnerving to stay in place. But Ace knew the group would discover them if they moved now.

He and Ailyn remained quiet and carefully watched when the intruder's lights suddenly turned away and flickered in an adjacent direction. The group didn't stop and soon were behind them, crossing their intersection point—the trail connected to a switchback right below them.

Ace whispered. "They shouldn't be able to see our footprints at night, but we'll grab our packs and go if they do."

One of the riders in the back stopped, leaving the motor running. The anticipation became overwhelming. Ace felt Ailyn's tension, knowing she wanted to get up and move.

They watched as he got off his ATV and stood sideways in the bright headlight. Ace could tell he was young, maybe in his early twenties. He was looking down at the ground. Ace held his pistol ready, unsure if the rider had spotted his and Ailyn's footprints. The young man stood still and urinated. He jumped back on the four-wheeler and sped off to catch up with the others.

Ace looked at Ailyn, seeing her wide-eyed and shaking in

fear.

"There's something you don't get to see every day," she said to cover her discomfort.

"You weren't looking, were you?" Ace chuckled and shook his head.

"No, no, I wasn't looking." They both smiled in relief. It took them a little time to relax and go back to sleep.

****

Ace awoke first, seeing the sun's earliest light creeping over the eastern horizon. He touched Ailyn's shoulder to wake her. They both began their morning rituals, making ready for a new day.

He applied another clean bandage and antibiotic cream on Ailyn's shoulder wound. "It's healing up pretty good. Is it still sore?"

"Not too bad today compared to yesterday."

"That's good; we're going to be okay, Ailyn!"

****

"Are you ready to go, honey? Slow and steady wins the race!" He stepped forward once more, setting the pace of the day like a deer hunter, stalking in for a closer shot.

She followed like it was a contest, and her skills improved as he heard less of her behind him but always sensed her closeness. Who could make less noise and still see the next danger sign? It became the new norm, and the couple stayed undetected and out of harm's way while challenging themselves and building their skills.

Toy Soldiers

(Day 3, 5:58 a.m.)

Minneapolis, MN

Much of Minneapolis was now on fire, turning the darkness into a red sky morning. No chance of the local weather station forecasting an approaching storm.

Two young men sat together on their back porch deck, watching the world around them fall into disarray. They started yesterday afternoon with two cases of Hamm's bottles on ice. Forty-four empties now stood tall before them, lined up like toy soldiers.

Reese and his friend Alger consciously decided to make the best of what could be their last days in an old reality. The details of their new existence were dim.

"Who would've ever thought something like this could happen in the United Fricken' States of America?" Reese said. He recalled spending time with his Dad in the woods and on camping trips. He wasn't sold on the survivalist lifestyle. When he was a student at the University of Minnesota, he put in just enough effort to pass and graduate. That was his form of survivalism. He was lucky to come from a long line of survivors, some of which had hardcoded into his genetics. He had a lack of interest, not of intelligence.

"Only four left, Alger," Reese opened two bottles with his favorite opener and passed one over.

"I gotta piss again!" Alger stood from his old porch chair and peed between the porch rails onto the ground below.

They saw a burning building crumbling in the distance, the sound taking a couple of seconds to reach them.

"Holy Shit, man!" Alger said in astonishment, not quite getting his zipper closed. "What are we going to do, Reese?"

"Right now, we're going to finish these beers. It could be a long time before we enjoy a case of the 'beer refreshing' together.

Reese thought again about his Dad. He knew he was probably already into phase two of his survival plan. He hoped his parents and his sister, Hatty, were okay. His dad used to tell him about each phase of his survival plan. He assumed they were already on their way to Mike and Sue's as he told him. "He always said this day would come," Reese said, realizing he had just shared his thoughts out loud.

"Who's that? Wait, what did he always say, Reese? Who are you talking about anyway?"

"My Dad."

"Here's to your Dad, Reese. He's a pretty cool Dad. I've always liked your old man." They clinked their bottles together and felt the need to chug them. "Two left!"

"Nah, let's get out of here. I've got a plan. We'll sacrifice these last two for my old man."

They grabbed their backpacks, pushed their bikes out the door, and carried them down the steps "Let's go hang out by the old mill, down by the river; I'm pretty sure, we can find a badass group to meet up with; maybe we'll even make it through this bullshit."

That was Reese's strategy when talking about survival with his Dad. He remembered the conversation like it was yesterday. "Yeah, Dad, I'll probably join some gang and do whatever it takes to get by." His dad didn't say it was a bad idea, so he was pretty sure he agreed with Reese. "Do whatever you've got to do to survive, Reese, whatever you have to do!"

Unanswered Questions

(Day 3, 6:03 a.m.)

New Elmar, WI

"Darin, do you think we should go to your Dad's bunker?" Hatty was becoming worried. They had gone three days without power and had no idea what had caused it. That just made everyone tense.

New Elmar, Wisconsin, is unincorporated. It had the obligatory bar on the corner of the county highway and a single country church with a cemetery. Two young families had moved into new homes built on the hill outside town.

Everything else was older and a little worn out. The townspeople had little desire to expand. There were several larger towns and cities within ten miles in almost every direction. It was quiet here, and people looked out for each other. Darin and Hatty both sensed that this was bigger than just a country power outage.

Darin's dad's old farm was a short walk from their home. A small assortment of organized farm machinery and vehicles sat at rest in the backyard behind the barn. Darin was mechanical. His off-road four-wheel-drive hobbies and winter snowmobile addiction had saved him and his family from boredom through all four Wisconsin seasons.

"No, not yet. We still have plenty of gas for the generator, so we can stay here at the house for a while," he said, hoping to ease her worries.

"Yeah, I guess I'm just paranoid. My Dad and I have talked about things like this happening. He warned me not to trust anyone. People can be dangerous when they're hungry or scared."

"It would be different if we lived in a big city, Hatty."

"Yeah, I can't even imagine what Minneapolis or La Crosse is like right now." She teared up thinking about her parents and her brother. She went over and hugged Darin for comfort. "I wish I knew if my Mom and Dad were okay, and Reese."

"It's okay, Hatty, I know; it's hard not being able to call

them."

He chuckled. "Your dad is a survivor, Hatty. He's been planning for this for years. If anybody can make it through shit like this, it's Ace. And you know your Mom will be right by his side. We'll be okay, Hatty, I promise."

Abe came down the stairs and smiled at his stepmother. "Good morning!" Looking into their faces, he could see their concern. "Is everything okay?"

"How did you sleep, buddy?" Hatty put her hands on his shoulders and gave him a quick peck on the cheek.

"Like a rock!" Abe was one of those resilient teens who didn't let things get to him. If he couldn't figure something out, he'd work through it and eventually ask for help. He listened to the generator behind the garage. "Dad, did you need me to refill the gas cans today?"

"Yeah, we better. Five cans of diesel should last until next Wednesday." Darin went to the steps and yelled, "Girls, it's time to get up; come on, we have a lot to do today!"

You could hear footsteps upstairs above the kitchen. Emma came down first. Even after a night's sleep, her long brown hair was barely out of place, and her face glowed without makeup. She was eighteen and looking forward to her last year of high school. Darin felt like it was just yesterday when she started kindergarten.

She was among the most popular girls in her class but didn't think much about it. She was similar to her stepmom. They were both blessed with a servant's heart and a continual desire to help others. She stood out from her peers with her natural confidence and grace.

She hugged Hatty first, resting her head on her shoulder. Her dad pushed her in the back with his hand.

"Don't…" She smiled at him.

"What?" He teased back.

She followed him to the sink and hugged him good morning as well.

The kitchen smelled like sizzling bacon and fried eggs.

Two fry pans on the stove. A pile of toast, all buttered and ready for Mama A's homemade strawberry jam sat on the island.

Hatty asked Emma to grab the plates and silverware. Breakfast was almost ready.

Annie was the last one to join everyone in the kitchen. She was the oldest of Darin's three children, home from college on break just before the power went down. She attended the University of Wisconsin in Oshkosh, majoring in graphic art.

Hatty thought back to when Darin first introduced her to his three kids. Annie accepted her right away. She and Hatty shared the oldest sibling roles in the families. As they grew closer, it was easy for Annie to share her challenges with Hatty.

"Hello, family." The tone in Annie's voice makes you wait for what she will say next—she is always funny. This time she quelled the humor and started a serious conversation. "Any idea yet if things are okay out there? It sucks not knowing what the heck is going on. Can we go see if Mom and Grandma are okay today?"

"Breakfast is ready; eat." Her Dad looked her in the eyes in an attempt to stay in the present.

"Here comes Josh and Penny, Dad!" Abe noticed them approaching before their dog even started barking. Their own dog followed along with them. Pretty soon, the sound of barking overtook the kitchen.

"Luna, quiet!" Darin commanded, slightly annoyed that Abe was better at guarding the house than the dog.

Josh knocked and opened the door. "Hi guys, how are you all doing?" Josh and Penny were great neighbors. They were about the same age as Darin and Hatty, and the two couples had cultivated a solid friendship.

"As good as we can be. Are you guys hungry?" Darin asked.

Josh told him they had just eaten, and Penny asked if they

had heard any more news.

"No, but I thought Abe and I would take the jeep to Paul and Becky Connelly's today. He's the only guy I know with a Ham radio. Maybe he can tell us what's happened. Would you stay here with Hatty and the girls while we're gone?" He asked.

"No problem," Penny said, looking back at Josh. She was glad to have the distraction and the girl's company.

"You want me to come with you guys?" Josh asked, not wanting to be left behind.

"Hey, come out and help me with something in the jeep," Darin needed time to explain his position privately. He would feel better if his friend stayed with his family in case anything happened. This new unknown required a stronger sense of responsibility for people's well-being. At least until after they know more about what's happened.

****

The county road south of town was open and looked the same. The father/son team came upon a stranded vehicle in the ditch on the right side of the road; they probably ran out of gas. The owner must have set off by foot to their destination.

They looked down the hill and saw several vehicles parked in the four-way intersection of Highway 23 and New Elmar Road. People stood together in small groups. They all turned to look at the sound of the jeep as it approached. John Steiner, an old high school classmate of Darin's, waved as he recognized the jeep. "Hi Darin, hey Abe!"

"Hey John, do you know what happened yet?"

"Yeah, I just got back from Connelly's. I was just sharing with everyone what Paul told me."

The rest of the group came over to the jeep. They were all familiar to Darin, but only by sight. He didn't know them very well.

John introduced him. "Hey everybody, this is Darin Knox

and his boy Abe. We went to school together." Once small greetings were exchanged, John continued.

"Paul told me that the Space Force took out the power and phone service. It's suspected that an internal terrorist organization is behind the whole thing."

"What? Seriously? Space Force?" Darin questioned the validity of his friend's story.

The small group discussed the likelihood of this and various plans if things worsened. One of the neighbors suggested meeting at this same intersection at noon daily so they could continue to gather and share information. John planned to visit Paul and Becky every morning and let the rest of the neighborhood know what he learned.

****

It didn't take long after saying goodbye to the group at the intersection to get back home. Hatty, Josh, and Penny met Darin and Abe by the jeep, and he told everyone what they had learned. While Darin wasn't as much a survivalist as his father-in-law, he grew up in a sustainable and hardworking farming family. He didn't take their current comfortable status lightly. They spent the rest of their day planning and preparing for any potential situation they could envision.

Hatty had learned many valuable lessons from her father, and she knew they needed to be ready for anything. Her Emergency Room nursing skills helped her work through worst-case scenarios. She prepared lists and delegated tasks to the kids to complete. This type of thinking proved helpful during the COVID-19 pandemic. Some people were paralyzed by fear and lost themselves and their usefulness to society. Their selfish hoarding caused others to go without. Darin would be willing to take the hard line for the benefit of his family if necessary. So would she, but her heart still led her to help those in need. She knew it had to be family first right now.

"Honey, I'm going to check on Evelyn, okay?" Hatty said to Darin. She was an elderly friend that lived just down the street. Evelyn reminded Hatty of Grandma and Nana Ayer. Women cut from the same cloth. Evelyn was in her mid-90s and had some recollection of World War II and the sacrifices families made to keep men on the frontlines and the US economy moving forward.

"Annie, go with her," Darin directed.

"Grab that Tupperware dish of left-over tuna salad, Annie. We can take that over with us."

"Okay, come on, Luna, come on, girl." Annie let her dog out, and the all-white German Shepherd bolted from her kennel. At seven, Luna was an excellent watchdog for her family. Annie missed her while away at college.

"See you in a little while. Love you." Hatty kissed her husband and stepped toward the door. Emma had that lost puppy look on her face, so Darin told her to go too. She jumped up off the island barstool and followed them out the door.

They approached the front door of Evelyn's home. Emma knocked. No answer. She knocked again. Again, no answer.

Hatty tried to open the door.

Annie looked through the window curtain next to the door and dropped the Tupperware dish. It hit the wood porch, the lid opened and spilled tuna salad everywhere.

"Hatty, Evelyn's lying on the floor!"

She looked through the window and saw her friend wasn't moving.

"Evelyn, wake up, Evelyn!" Knocking against the glass, but no movement. "Girls, go get your father, now!" She preferred they weren't there when she went into the house.

Hatty knew that her elderly friend was gone, recognizing the visible signs that she had expired. Her purplish skin tones could be seen through the window.

She lifted the edge of the porch flower pot and grabbed

the spare key. When the door opened, it was evident from the smell that her friend was dead, and she was too late to help her—feeling for a pulse and moving her onto her back. Her professional nursing experience took over. She pushed her emotions aside. Darin ran up the porch steps and met her inside.

"She's gone, Darin; keep the kids outside for me. Please open some windows and then go find Father Brillion at the church and ask him to come."

Hatty spent the next few hours prepping Evelyn's body the best she could for burial. No one left to call, as 911 was no longer an option. The job solely became her responsibility.

Hatty, Darin, the three kids, Josh, and Penny, stood in the parish's rural cemetery with Father Brillion. It was an unusual burial without a casket. The men respectfully wrapped Evelyn up in white sheets and then created a cocoon of plastic sheeting.

The funeral home in Kewaskum had recently dug a new gravesite at this cemetery and left the machinery behind. Darin and Abe hotwired the small backhoe and dug the grave together.

It was a solemn event. Evelyn's real family lived far from their beloved relative, making traveling and checking on her impossible. It was only Day 4 of these very uncertain times.

"Thank you, Father Brillion; at least we could give her a proper burial."

Yes, Hatty," he said. "She's at rest and doesn't have to experience any more troubling times."

"Are you doing okay, Father?" She asked. He was a younger Priest. They weren't members of his church but had gotten to know him a bit.

"Thank you, Hatty. It's kind of you to ask. I'm okay. Life is filled with challenges. So many things for us all to ponder. These are the times that can test even the most faithful. Don't let anything that happens call into question that God is still in control, Hatty. Keep your faith strong, and we will all get through this together. It was simply Evelyn's time to be called home."

Hatty smiled, agreed, and said, "Amen!"

Her Silhouette

Day 6, 4:46 a.m.

North Bend, WI

By the sixth day, Ace's life had turned upside down. He felt an awkwardness and unfamiliar anxiety that made it difficult for him to concentrate. He stopped and took a deep breath, trying to focus. Something else was wrong.

"Dan, stop for a second. I've got something in my shoe." Ace turned to look just as Ailyn leaned forward, and an arrow whizzed past directly over her head. The razor-sharp broadhead hit the tree behind and buried itself deep into the bark.

Suddenly, the woods came to life. Several birds took flight, and a squirrel ran to the cover of its family tree.

Instinctively tracing the arrow's flight, Ace brought his crossbow up to his shoulder as he spotted the hunter. He was attempting to nock another arrow. As the man started to draw back his compound bow for a second shot, Ace set his crossbow bolt free and hit the camouflaged tree stander directly in the neck. He was pinned upright against the tree, fighting for his last seconds of life, then his body hung limp.

In his death, the hunter's reflexes caused his fingers to relax; the second arrow fell to the ground, and then he dropped his bow.

While this hunter was no longer a threat, Ace wasn't convinced they were alone; he aimed his pistol and pivoted in every direction, listening and looking for signs of movement.

"Are you okay, Ailyn," he whispered between fast breaths.

"Yes," Ace heard her whimper; the near miss had shaken her.

It was gruesome to witness this man, lifeless, held up only by the strength of a carbon crossbow bolt through the center of his neck.

"We must be near a group," Ace said. "Start taking our gear up by that rock overlook, and wait for me. We'll hide there until dark and see if anyone comes looking for him."

****

Ace, heard the low hum of a UTV coming up from the valley floor north of the highway. The machine's lights made a zigzagging pattern. Two men followed the rugged trail to the top of the ridge where their comrade was found dead from an 'accidental' discharge of his compound bow. All usable light was disappearing around the elevated overlook.

The UTV stopped below the dead man's tree stand; its riders could see him hanging upside down from his safety harness. Ace hoped they couldn't assemble all the clues in the darkness.

Ace had climbed up on the metal stand and staged the scene, so it appeared the unfortunate hunter was the victim of equipment failure. A broken compound bow laid on the ground with a broken arrow stuck backward through the hunter's neck wound, looking like the compound bow had misfired.

Ace had carefully brushed any identifiable evidence of the encounter away using a branch with leaves, careful not to disturb the blood, underbrush, or leave any footprints behind.

He used the side of the hunter's ATV trail to exit the area, then stepped off at a calculated spot away from the tree stand and climbed up to Ailyn.

The rock cliff gave them cover and an excellent vantage point to view the hunter's friends when they found him at his staged accident scene.

The two men took a while to review and assess what had happened, not finding any flaws in Ace's masquerade.

They brought their friend's dead body down and laid him in the dump box of the UTV, unknowingly following through with the second half of Ace's plan. They stopped at a farmstead neither he nor Ailyn had noticed, allowing them to adjust their path forward to avoid further confrontation with this group.

Feeling relatively safe on the rock cliff, Ace was exhausted and needed to sleep. He slid into their sleeping bag, which Ailyn had laid over a bed of dry leaves. It felt soft, like a goose-down mattress. She was already asleep.

It had been a poor year for mosquitoes; sporadic rainstorms left the Driftless region with less standing water than normal.

Ace stayed awake, watching Ailyn. While she was a strong woman, she needed him. And he simply couldn't imagine his own life without her. *I need to keep her safe*, he thought. Had he sensed the danger before Ailyn leaned forward to take her shoe off, and the hunter unleashed his arrow? The fear of being found by the heavily armed men startled him back awake. Ace slowed his breathing and purposefully worked on calming his erratic heartbeat. He knew he needed to lean into his instincts; heeding those early internal warnings next time.

He counted backward from one hundred and fell back to sleep- seventy-nine, seventy-eight, seventy….

Peanut M&M’s

Day 7, 9:04 a.m.

North Bend, WI

As they got closer to the outer limits of North Bend, Wisconsin, Ace thought about how to best cross the Black River.

He had crossed earlier with Greg, and the bridge they used was an option, but they were still miles away from it. He started to look for a shallow spot. They walked along the banks, hugged against the edges so they could see the river, and still relied on the woodland cover.

****

Mike and Sue were blocked in and separated from the outside world.

He booby-trapped some funnel spots on his property with various methods perfected from his trapping experience, and off the internet.

He knew some people could fall prey to these dangerous and possibly lethal traps as they tried to invade his and Sue's safe zone. He accepted this as a new reality. These were troubling times, and there was only room for those he trusted completely. Ace, Ailyn, and Pete. They shared the same values, beliefs and concerns. This wasn't a numbers game; it was a survival game.

He figured Ace and Ailyn would make it to them first. Pete's arrival depended on whether he was in Sparta or La Crosse when the power went down. Ace and Pete both knew the safe entrance point to his property.

"I wonder how everybody's doing out there, Sue," Mike asked. "Ace and Ailyn could be here by Sunday."

"I hope so; it would be nice to have some company; and help. Ailyn and I haven't always been close, but she's a hard worker, and it would be nice to have another woman here for companionship."

****

Ace and Ailyn found shelter in an empty corn crib at the

edge of an alfalfa field about a hundred yards off the highway and the river. It was a perfect hiding spot. The crib's roof had holes, but it still seemed structurally sound. They wouldn't be visible to anyone from the highway. Tall burn thistle and burdock protected them from view. The open slat walls allowed them to monitor outside noise, and an exit door faced away.

"What's on the menu tonight, Ailyn?"

"I thought we better eat protein, so we'll have enough energy for tomorrow. We'll have dried fruit for breakfast with crackers and peanut butter."

"That sounds fine, but I've got a better idea!" Ailyn looked over at him, a little surprised. He lifted two-floor boards and placed them aside. Then he laid down on his belly, sticking his head and shoulders below the floor. He rummaged around until he found a silver-covered storage container.

"What the heck is in there?"

"I stashed this here about a year ago, just in case something like this ever happened." Ace opened the metal can and removed the contents.

"Oh my God, is that what I think it is?" She grabbed the vacuum-sealed yellow bag—a family-sized package of peanut M&M's; Ace smiled at her, knowing it was one of her favorites.

He pulled a miniature cook stove, a camper-sized saucepan, and metal spoons out of the can. He then opened a can of homestyle baked beans and a packet of dehydrated beef hamburger from inside his pack and then poured it all into the pan. The smell was amazing and comforting. It was their first hot meal since Bill's farm.

"I know it's not much, honey, but it'll be warm."

"No, no, it's perfect! Give me a spoon!" Ailyn thought about how thoughtful Ace was; they were getting worn out. A warm meal and her favorite candy boosted her spirits and gave her motivation to continue.

They ate until the saucepan was empty, and each ate another handful of M&M's for dessert. Ailyn yawned and rested her head softly on his shoulder. After another long day of walking, she was exhausted and fell asleep while he kept watch.

The couple took noise seriously; Ailyn had woken him several times over the past few nights to silence his snoring. Those sounds could lead to discovery. It could prove lethal if they both were down simultaneously. Neither had gotten more than five consecutive hours of sleep over the last two days of traveling. They continued to fight the urge to give up. Sleep deprivation played tricks on them. But they were both focused on survival and their goal to get to Mike and Sue's.

****

Mike was on a walk to check the punji sticks on his property—camouflaged from the sight of most unknowing intruders.

He crested over the hillside and saw something was in a trap. As he approached, he could see a small nubby buck pinned backward against a tree with its head down and no life left in its torso.

The sharpened wooden sticks had penetrated its young body, and it appeared that one of the points made a perfect heart shot. The young deer had expired quickly.

He was a sportsman with a wall full of trophy heads and shoulder mounts. His motto was always. 'Let em go so they can grow!' The fresh meat would supplement their food stores, but he was sorry his trap had taken down the young buck.

Mike removed the traps restraints, and the deer fell to the ground. He carefully removed it with his handmade sumac walking stick. Bloody points showed red in the green underbrush, so he used old leaves to clean them off and reset the trap.

"I think I'll field dress you out behind the pole barn," he said, realizing he had just spoken aloud to a dead deer. As Sue said, having more company at the house would be good. "Sue, fresh venison for dinner," he called out, dragging the small animal down the hill to the pole barn door.

"Oh my God, how did you get that deer? I didn't hear you shoot?"

"He ran into one of my traps. I knew it could happen, but only to young ones like this. A big buck would be too smart to get close to a trap set with my scent on it."

"Oh, it's a nubby, too bad," she said. "Give me the inner loins, and I'll make them up with some canned corn and potatoes for supper."

"Mmmm, that sounds great; I'll start butchering once I check the rest of the property. Now that I know this can happen, I'll have to check the traps every day." Mike prepared the deer, hanging it up in the pole barn. Sue got busy setting everything out for him to butcher. When finished, he could leave the remains, and coyotes would clean them up in a few days.

Mike returned to the shed. It took a few hours to skin and debone the carcass. The cooler was half full and easy to carry into the house.

He reasoned that it must have been a springtime birth; there wasn't much meat on this one. Best of the land, though, as it may be the most tender venison meat the couple has ever enjoyed together. They could get maybe twenty good meals for two, less if they needed to share.

****

Ace and Ailyn would take turns; one would sleep while the other kept watch. Ace lost track of the days. He would cipher which day it was by remembering past events. He believed today was day eight.

They had suffered only a single lethal incident thus far in their journey through hiding and avoidance. They hadn't experienced any retribution from the hunter's 'accident.'

They didn't know for sure, but Ace guessed they had it much easier than the rest of the country. If the government held any functionality, it was only in critical areas. He believed most cities across the country had most likely fallen into chaos. Martial law would become the only organizational hierarchy.

Sleep was a welcome escape from reality. But they only enjoyed brief catnaps at best. Thoroughly exhausted, Ailyn dreamt of Christmas past. Happy times spent with family. Hatty and Reese, little again, innocent and full of hope.
Ailyn woke in fear for their wellbeing, realizing she had accidentally fallen asleep on her watch. Dan was startled awake and jumped to his feet, pulling his sidearm. When they identified they were safe, they both settled back and snacked on more M&M's. "I'm worried about Hatty and Reese, Dan. I can't take it anymore. I have to know if they're safe."

"Okay, Honey, calm down, it's alright. You fell asleep and must have had a nightmare."

"No, it was Christmas, and we were all together. The kids were still small."

"Then I guess you were just worried about them, and it woke you up."

"Yeah, I guess so."

"I have an idea, something my grandmother shared with me. An experience she had once. Let's try it together, okay?"

Ailyn nodded.

"Let's see if I can remember how she explained it! Lay down here and stretch your arms out toward the kids, this way and that way, I think. Right hand for Hatty and left for Reese. I'll lie next to you and do the same thing. We close our eyes, and in our minds, keep saying their names until they are both standing right above us. If we do it together, they will sense us and know we are thinking about them.

Okay, are you ready? Start saying their names in your mind."

Ailyn spoke their names to herself, "Hatty, Reese, Hatty, Reese, Hatty, Reese, Hatty, Reese." Suddenly they both were above her.

"Talk to them, Ailyn, quietly and calmly talk to them," he whispered. Tell them anything you want to share with them." Dan felt Ailyn's body tense.

She spoke to them in her mind, a conversation that brought great peace and love to her heart. *Kids, I love you both so much. I'm sorry the world has come to this. Please survive! Do whatever you have to do to survive. I love you so much. We are heading to Mike and Sue's like your Dad said we would. If things return to normal, you will know where to find us. Take care of yourselves, and know we will always love you to the moon and back!*

****

Hatty awoke from sleep.

She felt overwhelmed with love and affection, but started to cry.

"Hey, Babe, are you okay?" Darin woke up asking, concerned.

"I just saw my Mom and Dad lying on a wooden floor. They are alive. They're okay, Darin, and they are trying to communicate with me. Oh my God, Darin, they're okay!"

****

Reese and a small group of his new friends were about to go out on an early morning collection mission.

Noticing the strange look on his face, Alex asked, "Hey, what's up, Reese?"

"I'm not sure. That was weird! I just thought about my parents. I saw them both lying together with their eyes closed. I think they were trying to tell me they were okay!"

"Cool, like ESP? Are you a psychic, man?"

Uncomfortable, Reese shrugged it off and changed the

subject. But inside, he felt his parent's love, which made the burden of survival a little lighter.

****

Ailyn opened her eyes, and Dan saw her looking at him in the moonlight; he smiled. "I feel better, Dan. I was with them, and they knew it! And they feel how much I love them both."

"They know, Honey, they know! Everything's going to be okay!"

Ailyn smiled, knowing he was doing it again. Dan, always knew not just when but how to reassure her. It worked, at least temporarily. Sometimes the extra effort only delayed the inevitable, but she appreciated him very much at that moment.

"Let's both try and get some more sleep; we'll start hallucinating if we don't." Squeezing Ailyn's hand, he said. "I'll try and stay up for a little while until you fall asleep again."

"We're hidden pretty well. We both can sleep at the same time," Ailyn whispered. "Who would think to look in this old corn crib anyway?"

Ailyn fell asleep first; her dreams went right back to the kids. It was Thanksgiving, 2018. It was their last holiday together in the kid's childhood home, an apartment they lived in before moving into the new house.

Games, food, and celebration! Stuffed bellies and rental movies. All the dogs were running around the house. It made for a fun day that she wished could last forever. Embracing the snapshots of joy in her heart; and those lasted forever.

Her dreams took a macabre twist. The two men she had shot reappeared with them in their apartment. They were invading her happy memories. She reshot them-this time in front of her family. Everything went wrong. Her dreams and feelings moved from love, joy, and happiness to terror and anxiety.

She awoke and gasped for air. Once again, holding her, Ace whispered that she was okay. "It's only a dream, honey, just a dream. It'll get light in about an hour. Let's skip sleep for now. We'll cross over to the edge of this field and get back to cover by the river. Let's pack up, and we'll make our way over there before it gets any lighter." Ailyn was shaky and tired.

They safely descended the banks to the tree cover and stopped at a comfortable spot, eating the last dehydrated apple slices, peanut butter, and walnuts from Ailyn's pack. The skyline was brightening. It was going to be a clear and sunny day.

Ace wasn't sure, but he felt they may have slept another two hours. But it wasn't restorative, and Ailyn struggled with all that had happened. It was starting to wear on him mentally as well.

"How much water do we have left in the filter bottles," he whispered. "We better fill them up when we get the chance."

Ailyn's hand straightened out, Pointing her index finger up in the air for him to stop and listen. "Shhhh...... listen," Ailyn froze. There were sounds coming from downstream. The water was pretty shallow at this time of the year. "There," she mouthed, pointing to a canoe, a woman paddling in front and a man in the back. They slowly moved upstream against the current, skirting close to the opposite bank. They had a fair amount of gear covered and strapped down in the center of the canoe.

Ace touched Ailyn's shoulder and shook his head, knowing she wanted to stand and wave them over.

When the couple was about a hundred yards upstream and out of earshot, Ace whispered. "I know you wanted to help them, Ailyn, but we can't trust anyone."

"But they seem just like us, trying to get somewhere safe."

"I know; I'm sorry. But I have a plan," He explained.

"We'll use them as bird dogs. We can stay back on this side of the river to watch them from a safe distance. Any sign of trouble upstream, they experience it first." He saw a dark look pass over Ailyn's face. "The world is no longer fair. You have to trust me for this to work, okay?"

"I do."

"We'll go slowly; when they stop, we stop, when they paddle, we quietly move forward, okay?" She nodded again.

They drew nearer to the Hwy V Bridge west of North Bend. That would be the best to keep from crossing directly in the water, but neither knew how dangerous the bridge crossing would be that close to town properties.

Ace lost sight of their point guards on the water and needed to figure out where they went. He raised his hand in the air, demonstrating the universal signal for stop. Ailyn recognized the sign and froze. He found them across the river, standing inside the tree line. They were being watched through the scope of the man's rifle. Ailyn quickly hid behind cover, and Ace followed.

Ace peered around the tree trunk as the couple started pulling their canoe farther into the wood line away from the river, out of sight, showing a clear strategic advantage.

The north bank, closest to the highway, had all the houses and cabins. Ace heard voices further up the bank.

"Shit," Ace said. "Ailyn, come on, follow me." He knew it was a chance to take, but he saw no other options. They ran double-time, backtracking their steps in retreat, quickly putting a hundred yards between them and their would-be attackers.

They had run around a bend in the riverbank. It wouldn't take locals long to track and catch them if they had been seen.

"We need to cross the river now!" The open sand bar made it easy to run most of the way across, but Ace knew the deeper water would be on the outer bank. If they could get to the other side; they would be able to find suitable cover and fight back if they had to.

Suddenly a shot echoed through the river basin, then another, then quick bursts from a semi-auto. It sounded like an AR-15. Ace recognized the sound. Many of his friends owned them and enjoyed target practicing together on his old land.

The shooting stopped as they waded into the deeper water. Ace helped his wife, knowing her swimming skills were weak. The water was over their heads, so he pulled her a short distance and let her know when it was safe to stand up again.

They climbed the steep bank and escaped unseen. Heading into the tree line, Ace noticed Ailyn looking upstream. They made eye contact with the canoe woman.

All hell broke loose again. A firefight went on for minutes!

Ace and Ailyn kept running through the plowed furrow of an almost fully-grown bean field. The shooting stopped as they reached the other side.

A barbed-wire fence on top of a long pile of fieldstones was one more obstacle between them and safety. The fence was neglected, broken between its rusty metal posts. They made their way down into the underbrush of an enormous sinkhole filled with thickets—a small clearing at the bottom to stop and catch their breath.

"Are you okay?" Ace whispered.

They were soaking wet from head to toe, and Ailyn started to shiver.

"Let's get out of these wet clothes and dry off."

Still shaken, she pulled open her sealed pack and grabbed a dry towel with trembling hands. They took turns drying each other off and crawled into their sleeping bag.

The warmth felt like security. Another welcome escape from reality. They fell asleep in each other's arms.

Neither of them cared anymore. They were exhausted, with no energy left to flee or fight, total surrender.

Old Sturgis

Day 9, 2:46 p.m.

North Bend, WI

After a few hours of sleep, the couple was startled awake by more gunfire. They quickly got up and broke camp. Both were exhausted, but they pressed on. Now that they were walking on the southern side of the Black River, they would have the opportunity to stop at another old friend's house. While they were no longer on Ace's original route, this detour might provide a safe spot to stay overnight and rest. Maybe they would be able to even restock. Ace was concerned about what kind of reception they would receive; they were unexpected and a walk up unannounced from the river bottoms seemed aggressive.

Ace's friend Wayne was born and raised on this land. He let Ace and Reese hunt for deer there, and that experience helped navigate the confusing network of run-offs and tributaries.

They would have to make at least one more water crossing, but hopefully, with low water levels, they could do it without getting their clothes wet again.

"Do you hear that, Ailyn? It sounds like an ATV is running."

Wayne's farm dog had already sounded the alarm. They weren't out of the bottoms yet, and the dog knew they were there. Ace sensed that Wayne might have his rifle and scope pointed in their general direction, scanning for a clean shot. He wanted to get Wayne's attention and find a way to identify themselves before he could get a shot off. But first, they needed to cross.

"I'll take off my boots and roll up my pants, Ailyn. Then I'll cross with all the gear and comeback to get you. You can piggyback over with me so we can stay dry."

They made it safely to the other side. He was a little soggy, but Ailyn and their gear were dry. He was happy it was going well. He thought more about how they could let

Wayne know it was them. He had an idea.

"Take my cut out of my pack, Ailyn, and give it to me."

The two men had been in recovery together. They rode with the same sober motorcycle group. "I need to show Wayne something familiar so he doesn't shoot us."

"Wayne, it's Ace and Ailyn, don't shoot!" Ace called out. He waited, hoping for a reply. No response.

Ace called out again, lifting his leather vest above his head to show the different patches. "Wayne, are you up there?" Still nothing.

The running motor's sound got louder as they walked towards Wayne's pole barn home. Ace thought it was just idling.

As he turned around the corner of the tan-colored pole barn home, Ace immediately knew something was wrong. He saw the red ATV and Wayne lying on his belly on the ground. Sturgis, his companion dog, sat by his side, waiting for a command, protecting his master.

Ace couldn't stop Ailyn from turning the corner. She screamed when she saw his body in the gravel. They ran to Wayne. Ace turned his old friend onto his back. His fingers felt along Wayne's dark red neck for a pulse. "Wayne, wake up. Wayne, are you alright?" Ace said, shaking him. He didn't have a pulse. The noise from the running motor became a distraction, so Ace reached up and turned off the ignition key in the center of the handlebar.

Sturgis got up and moved closer to Ace, nudging him gently with his furry head. His natural response was to reassuringly pet the dog's ear and neck. When he touched Wayne's neck and hands, they were cool to the touch.

"Ailyn, Wayne's dead." He felt once more for a pulse just to make sure.

Overcome with exhaustion and sadness, Ailyn broke down. Tears streamed down her cheeks as she wiped them away with her shirt sleeve. "Did he have a heart attack,

Dan?"

"Geez, I don't know. It looks like it, maybe, yes."

Sturgis began licking Wayne's face. "Come here, Sturgis, come here, boy," Ailyn said.

"Can we give him a proper burial; we can do that for him, right?"

"Yeah, but how?"

Wayne's diesel skid steer, was parked near the cow barn entrance, the key left in the ignition. It easily broke ground to create a long channel along the top of the hill in front of a big picture window. Wayne appreciated his view of the Black River winding its way through the bottomlands. Ace felt it was a perfect place for his friend's final resting place.

They worked together to place him in a respectful and peaceful position. "I'm so sorry, Wayne," Ace said, rubbing his eyes. "Forgive me for not getting here sooner."

Ailyn found Wayne's colors from a closet in the house and had properly folded them. She handed them down into the shallow grave, where Ace gently laid them over Wayne's chest.

"God, please help bring him home to you," Ace heard Ailyn pray.

Ace used the skid steer to cover the body. He was filled with emotion and grief. He would miss his dear friend.

After a few moments of silence, Ailyn asked, "What should we do now, Dan?"

"I'm going to leave a note behind for his family, telling them where Wayne's body is buried. Maybe it will give them some peace?" Ace sat down at the kitchen table and began to write.

Dear Roger and family

I'm so sorry.
I crossed the Black River to get to your Dad's and found him

unresponsive on the gravel driveway.
I'm not certain what happened; it looked like maybe he had a heart attack.
I used the skid steer to dig a grave, and placed him under the picture window so he's overlooking the bottoms.
I'm so sorry. I'm making my way south.

Prayers to you all,
Ace

Ace considered using Wayne's ATV to travel east to Mike and Sue's. It was tempting, but would be dangerous. It was similar to how tricky it was for him and Greg when they used the dirt bikes. By now, people wouldn't hesitate to pick off a moving target just to steal stuff. Staying on foot was still the safest option. Ace guessed they were still at least a few days away from Mike and Sue's. But there were enough connecting woods along the river bottoms to keep them hidden and away from people.

Sturgis laid down at the front of Wayne's grave and whimpered. "Come on, Sturgis. Let's go, buddy, come here, Sturgis." Sturgis's loyalty and sadness prevented him from leaving his master.

It was nearing the end of day nine.

Molotov Cocktail

Day 10, 7:53 p.m.

Minneapolis, MN

Reese and Alger had joined with the forming group at the Pillsbury Museum. Alger decided to go on his own to his girlfriend's apartment. It didn't take Reese long to become close friends with Alex and Liam. They were his kind of people; down to earth and fun. Once he'd settled in a little bit, he shared his thoughts on heading over to a store up the street. The person that seemed to be in charge, Karla, liked the idea.

Six members of the small museum group climbed the steps to the sixth floor of the Minneapolis outlet store. They had decided together to start at the top and work their way down to the main floor, scavenging for survival items.

"Reese over here, look what I found!" said Karla, his newest friend and original founding member of his new group, 'The Millers.'

She was physically fit, and he was very attracted to her. His type. The kind of girl he liked to meet at a bar near closing time. Maybe it was because now she used her makeup as camouflage instead of vanity.

"Holy shit Karla, you've found the mother lode of long underwear." Reese smiled at her, a trace of sarcasm in his voice.

She threw a pair back at him. "When it's negative fourteen this January, and you're freezing your nuts off, I'll ask if you have a pair of these bad boys on?"

"Ha, no, Karla, I'm serious, great find. How many do you think you can carry in your backpack?" Reese quickly spoke, changing the conversation back in his favor. He liked her and didn't want to offend her. *'Really, Reese,'* he thought to himself, *'you're going to blow this over long johns?'*

They heard gunfire and glass breaking on the other side of the store. They quickly crouched down and hid behind an aisle kiosk. The muzzle flashes lit up the darkened sixth floor. One of the men yelled, "This is our store, give yourselves up now!"

"Are they coming this way?" Karla whispered as they kept out of sight.

Reese peered over a stack of multi-colored water bottles. Alex, Liam, Bjorn and Peter were pinned down and had little chance of escape.

'Freeze, flee, or fight' came to Reese's mind. He thought of his Dad. '*What should I do, Dad*?' He almost spoke the thought.

Neither he or Karla had the firepower capable of protecting themselves against semi-automatic weapons. But Karla had two small Molotov cocktails safely wrapped inside her pack; she pulled them out and showed them to Reese.

"Reese, if we get closer, we can throw these. It'll cause a distraction, so we can all run for the stairs!"

Very quietly and carefully, Reese led Karla to the right side of the store, strategically positioning them behind the two shooters. He was surprised and impressed by her preparedness. "Hand me one," he whispered.

She handed the glass over and held hers up next to his and, pulling a lighter out of her pocket, lit the cloth draped down the side of each pint-sized mason jar.

The flames lit up the immediate area. Karla and Reese looked at each other and simultaneously threw the makeshift bombs directly at the shooters.

The jars hit the hard flooring, shattering as the gasoline burst into flames. Both shooters were engulfed by gasoline and fire.

The gunshots stopped as the shooters ran screaming through the outerwear section; the clothing racks lit up as they spread fire in every direction.

The main stairwell exit from the sixth floor was impassable as the room filled with flames and smoke.

"Karla, let's go!" he started pulling her toward the exit sign on the other side of the store.

“Hey, you guys, follow us. Is anybody hurt?” Karla yelled over the sounds of the growing inferno. Miraculously all four of their remaining crew stood up and ran to them. The shooters had stopped running and lay on the ground; the only other movement was the dancing fire and smoke.

Reese and Karla didn’t have time to think about what they had done. They needed to make sure everyone in their group got out safely. Later, they would need to come to terms with their actions. But it was a kill-or-be-killed situation. “Here, Karla, this way.” The sign shone bright, a beacon that read ‘Emergency Exit.’ Eight people were in the building, but only six pushed through the steel fire door.

The stairs were dark. Karla peeled back the tip of a road flasher she carried and scratched it against the cap. It flashed white like a giant sparkler. The stairwell lit up, and they made a rapid descent.

On the way down, Reese looked out the fourth-floor window and saw the reflection of their building on the glass panel wall of the bank across the street.

“Hey, look!” They all stopped for just a moment to watch as the flames engulfed their building’s top floor. It looked like a giant candlestick mirroring the fire’s reflection up and down Hennepin Avenue.

Karla stopped everyone at the bottom of the steps. “Wait, hold on. Don’t just blow out the door.” She slowly opened the emergency exit door and peeked outside, looking in all directions. “Looks clear.” She held the door as everyone made their way out into the street.

They ran alongside the abandoned shops and businesses that pre-COVID once had thrived and prospered. They turned right and ducked into the darkened security of a one-way alleyway.

Reese looked back; no one had followed them. But he was left with memories. He moved to the front and told his friends about his old apartment off 10th Street.

He found himself in a co-leadership position with Karla.

"I know a bunch of shortcuts back to the mill."

They all had full backpacks, with enough long johns to last their group a lifetime, and other essentials to aid them in their survival efforts.

"This way, we can hide here and take a break. I've got a few things I'd like to grab and take back to the mill with us." The alley behind Reese's apartment was dark. The only light was coming from the burning Marx building, lighting up the skyline.

"We can go in the back door." It was just as he and Alger had left it a week ago. The two unopened Hamm's beer bottles stood guard over the small army of empties standing upright in parade formation.

Reese thought about his friend Alger, did he make it to his girlfriends? He hadn't seen him since and hoped he was alright. Karla quickly interrupted the thought, "You going to open the door? I've got to pee!"

Alex asked, "Reese, do you mind if we tap these last two beers?"

"First door on the right past the kitchen," he called out to Karla. Reese hesitated to answer Alex's request. He had mixed feelings about these guys drinking the memorialized beer. He took a double breath and said, "Yeah, go ahead, but they're probably piss warm."

"Let's all take a hit off them to celebrate!" Bjorn said.

"Warm or not, they're gonna taste great," Alex said. He pulled a speed blade from his pocket that hung from his car keys.

'*Here's a man after my own heart; he carries a mini,*' thought Reese."Karla, you want a swig of this," Reese asked, reaching the bottle toward her as she returned from the bathroom.

"No, I don't drink," she answered back.

"Ever?" He surprisingly replied.

She seemed uncomfortable, so he spoke out to her again. "My mom and dad don't drink either. My dad hasn't drank since 1980."

"No shit? I've been sober since 2016," she replied. "Did they go to meetings?"

"They used to, but I'm not sure they have them anymore?" He said jokingly but then realized it was dumb to say under the circumstances.

She looked down and away, annoyed by the topic and explanation.

"That's okay, Karla," Reese said. "I'll make this my last one, and from now on, we'll do it together, okay?"

She glanced up at him with affection and a smile.

He thought it was probably like the look on his dad's face when his mom took her last drink in support of his sobriety. "Besides, if it isn't ice cold, it's not worth drinking, right Alex?"

"Oh, I don't know about that, dude. I'll finish yours if you don't want it."

Changing the subject, Liam asked, "Should we stay here tonight?"

"That sounds like a good idea; make yourselves at home, guys! Whatever's mine is now yours. I'm not going to wait on any of you!"

Peter and Alex started opening the cabinets in the kitchen. "Is this what I think it is, Reese?" Alex cried out, holding up a dark red colored mason jar.

"Yeah, it's my Mom's homemade spaghetti sauce."

Liam and Bjorn were in the living room looking around at Reese's stuff and quickly returned down the hallway, "Let's have spaghetti!"

"See if I have any noodles. I doubt it."

"What's this?" Alex had two more jars of canned goods in his hands.

Reese answered. "Canned potatoes and venison."

"No shit!" Alex replied. "I can cook all of this if we find a way to warm it up."

"Heck yeah, we're going to have ourselves a feast

tonight," Bjorn said.

"How can we warm it up?" Alex asked.

"Peter, there's a camping stove in that closet by you, and there's a big saucepan under the stove."

They heard a loud crash as the group opened the mason jars and mixed the ingredients into the pan.

Reese moved to the back door and opened up the shade. All he could see was dust and smoke coming from the downtown area. It reminded him of the store they had just been in.

"Nice job Karla; see what you did to that nice building!" Reese teased.

Karla quickly shot back, giggling. "Shut up, Reese. You threw the other Molotov cocktail, so it's just as much your fault."

"Okay," he said, "we did it together then!" The two fist-bumped and exploded their hands open in the air. They were starting to establish their interest in each other. The four other men knew that Karla was officially off-limits. Reese had staked a claim.

"Fire that Coleman up, you guys. Let's break some bread. After dinner, I have a little treat for us!"

"As if it could get any better than this, Reese," Alex said as the smell of food overtook them in the dirty kitchen.

They ate by candlelight in the living room. No one was worried about doing the dishes. Only time would tell if tonight would become one they looked back on fondly.

Alex sat back in his seat and rubbed his belly, stuffed from their hot meal.

Reese stood up from the room's power chair, went to his bedroom, and opened a box next to his nightstand. Noise from a cellophane bag crinkled in his hands. He walked back into the living room.

"Would anyone like a Lindon chocolate?" He smiled and passed the bag to Karla.

She didn't have to say a word. The look on her face was

priceless joy.

"Can you believe this guy?" Liam said aloud.

"Reese, this is the best night we've had since the power went out," Peter stuffed a piece of chocolate into his mouth and spoke while still chewing. "We might not have made it out of that building alive if it wasn't for you and Karla; thank you, guys!"

"Yeah, thanks, guys!" It was an emotional moment between new friends who would share this special bond forever, like soldiers after battle.

Humbled, Reese stated, "Karla had the gas bombs stashed in her pack. I didn't even know she had them until the shots started. She's the one we should all be thanking."

"Maybe we should all try to get some sleep." Karla uncomfortably changed the subject.

"I'm exhausted, and now I've got a food hangover. It won't be sleep; it will be a food coma," Peter said with another mouth full of chocolate.

"My old roommates' room is on the right, and two can stay on the couches; you guys figure it out, okay? Karla and I are going to take my room."

"Oh, we are, are we?" She said, "I always sleep on the right side of the bed."

****

Reese's eyes opened, sensing the warm body next to him. Daylight peeked through the side slits of the old dusty blanket that covered the bedroom window. Smoke clouds occasionally blocked it.

People had been leaving the inner city since 2020, but the most recent departures were probably trapped in the suburbs, enduring their new chaos, unaware of what was coming next.

The people who had decided to stay or simply couldn't leave were either in hiding or caught up in the middle of gang warfare—fighting for territory, rich with supplies, increasing their long-term means of survival.

Reese thought of those groups as Metros. And holding strong against the Metro's was a significant challenge. He knew from their encounter his group was unfairly disadvantaged. The Millers had grown to almost thirty strong in ten days but still paled in size to the Metros. They made the old Pillsbury Mill museum their home and carved out the west side of the river up Hennepin Avenue and over to 7th Street as their territory. They were lucky to have made it out of that building alive. Two shooters with semi-automatic weapons would easily have killed all six of them without those cocktails. Luckily, they had gone up in flames instead.

Reese was concerned that it could be only a matter of time before the old mill museum would fall. If a quick decision was necessary, what would he need to do? Who did he want to come with him? How could they escape to a safer place outside of the city?

Looking down at Karla lying comfortably in his bed instinctively changed him from a "me" to a "we." He felt an unfamiliar sense of commitment in his young heart. It could be far worse; she had skills, and he admired that independence and ingenuity. Where and how did she acquire her survival knowledge?

"Karla, wake up," he said softly.

"I'm awake," opening and then closing her eyes several times to adjust to the light from the window. "What's up, Reese?"

"The mill. We're not prepared to fight off a major attack."

"Yeah, I know; I thought about that too. Got any ideas?"

"I was thinking about floating the river downstream to escape the city."

"Don't you think we would run into more people trying to do the same thing?" She replied casually.

"Yeah, I know, that's the other problem. Maybe we should try to make a truce with the Metros and join them.

There is strength in numbers. No reason why they wouldn't want to increase their size."

"How can we make that happen, though?" No one had taken a lead role yet, except Karla. All the forward movement the group had accomplished had occurred with little to no organization. Karla admired Reese's thinking and felt good that he had included her in his thoughts. She instinctively felt trust in this new partnership, but she remained cautious.

"Let's get back to the mill and have a meeting!"

They were the only ones up. Reese's apartment provided everyone with a temporary short-term sanctuary from this new harsh world. Not so long ago everyone was living their lives with structure and routine, goals and dreams. A false sense of security.

"Let's look around and decide if we should take anything else back."

Eventually, everyone started to wake up as Reese and Karla started looking through cupboards and drawers, and closets, trying to find things that may be helpful.

Peter called first dibs on pissing in the un-flushable, over-abused toilet.

Bjorn and Liam walked down the short hallway and joined them in the kitchen. "What's the plan, man?" Liam asked while yawning.

"We are looking for anything useful that we can carry back with us. Let's get everybody together and decide what to do when we get back to the mill." Reese didn't want to share what he and Karla discussed until they were all together. Karla had her secrets. She had served two deployments in Afghanistan as a Marine. She wasn't going to share this until it became necessary to share it.

Reese knew she had some formal training; she carried herself well and was highly aware of her surroundings. He wanted to ask but wasn't sure how. He didn't want to ask in front of everyone else. It felt too personal.

"Karla, I have something in the back corner of my closet you should carry. They went back into his room together and reached around the open bi-fold door of his closet. He grabbed a loaded hunting rifle and handed it to Karla.

"Well, will you look at this little beauty?" She handled the weapon with perfect control.

She opened the bolt, and the 30-06 shell ejected. It flipped in the air and landed on the blankets of the bed. Then she chambered another round and removed the clip to return the bullet to its proper spot.

"It's my deer rifle," Reese said. He knew she already knew that.

"Are you a hunter, Karla? Or were you in the Army?"

She looked at him and paused, making a split-second decision to give him her secret, "Marines, right out of high school."

"You're a badass. That's hot!"- he said with a smile.

"Ha, you got a thing for Marines? Or just strong females?"

"You should meet my Mom!" He said back quickly and laughed.

They smiled at each other with mutual admiration; nothing more needed to be said. Karla slung Reese's deer rifle over her shoulder and grabbed the half-spent box of shells from the floor. Brushing past him in the doorway, she smiled at him again, appreciating the new gift. She felt like giggling; this meant more to her than traditional tokens used to earn feminine affection: jewelry, flowers, well-planned dates.

"Hey guys, let's go. I'm ready to get back to the mill." Karla walked out of the room in front of Reese.

"Holy shit Karla, what's up with the gun?" Alex asked, a little shocked when he saw it over her shoulder.

"Reese just gave it to me for my birthday!"

"Wait, what? Is it your birthday today?" Reese asked,

surprised.

Karla hooked her finger into the edge of her mouth so she looked like a fish on a line.

Everybody laughed, including Reese, “Alright, good one. When is your birthday anyway?” Reese asked as they walked out the front door and down the steps.

“It was last night.” She smiled at him over her shoulder and gave him a wink. Reese was surprised to feel himself blush a little.

Now that they were back outside, they needed to stay alert and focused. They hurried across the abandoned street to the alleyway behind the ‘SandBox’ diner. The streets were empty; Minneapolis was a ghost town during the day.

Previously, it was a bustling, busy city. Literally overnight, it had become a place where people worked hard to remain unseen.

Burnt Chemical Smell

Day 11, 7:13 a.m.

Melrose, WI

The advantage of owning acreage on top of the tallest hillside in the county was the ability to see what was coming on the horizon.

After two more days and arriving at Mike and Sue's bunker, Ace knew it was time to go underground. As the light faded and the skies darkened, the two couples stood outside the bunker door and watched as everything in the storm's path became enveloped by smoke mixed with fire. It was monumental destruction.

"Do you hear that? It sounds like a dog barking," Ace said. He pointed to the field's edge, and they watched Sturgis moving at full speed, working hard to outrun the blowing debris. "It's Wayne's dog, Sturgis! He must have followed our scent from Wayne's farm," Ace said.

Ace began coughing as he opened the gray steel bunker door, and Sturgis ran inside and hid deep against the back wall of the inner room. As he settled in, he yelped and whined a bit. He was shaking. He rushed Ailyn and Sue inside, and Mike followed him in, closing and securing the sealed door behind him.

Because they had prepped well, this underground bunker had air and water filtration. They built it for the long haul and were prepared to ride out any catastrophe. Neither Ailyn nor Sue was fully aware of the measures they took to prepare for this anticipated yet unplanned situation.

"Sue, go to the breaker box and turn on the power!" Mike called out to her from the cement stairwell.

"Okay, got it!" she said. "Ailyn, did you know about this bunker before the power went down?"

"No, I didn't," she softly replied. "I used to make fun of Dan's survival talk, but now I'm glad he didn't listen to me."

Mike and Ace had several critical life support systems in place. Footstep power generating floor tiles and two bicycles charged the battery banks that supplied power to vital equipment and living amenities.

Ace and Ailyn's fitness would be invaluable for this daily responsibility as they had bicycled hundreds of miles a month together before the chaos. Mike and Sue held their own in other necessary tasks.

"Looks like you and Ailyn made it just in time!" Mike said.

"Yeah, I'm glad we weren't still out there. Whatever that was would have killed us. Come here, Sturgis. You're one lucky dog, boy." He moved tight against Ace's leg and received his reward; Ace knew all the good places dogs liked to be petted.

While Mike was closing and locking the sealed entrance door of the bunker, he coughed too. The wind was nearing hurricane speeds and horizontally blew debris past the doorway. Visibility had gone from ten miles to ten feet when the storm hit. Both men noted it smelled manufactured, with no familiar scents of dirt and ozone. Instead, it had a burnt chemical smell.

"Have you given any thought to a timeline?" Ace asked his friend.

"About staying down here? I think it will be at least eight months before it's safe. The winter elements will remove many of the impurities in the air. Spring will repair damage caused by the lack of sunlight and cold."

"Okay, I agree. What do you think that smell was?"

"I'm not sure. I'm glad we installed the hydro-air and water filtration system instead of adding another solar bank. The panels will probably be useless now."

"We will make it through this together. I'll talk with Ailyn later so she understands what's at stake. This will be difficult for all of us. We'll do our best, Mike!"

"I know, Buddy! I'm not sure how we'll feed the dog, though. Table scraps, I guess."

Both couples were safe, hunkered down inside their underground bunker. No one knew what had made the sky dark, but they all assumed it was nuclear.

Like everyone else in the U.S., no one knew each other's fates unless they were with friends and family. They didn't know who was still alive, who had perished, and who was at risk. Nor did they know what would happen to themselves. Would they have enough food and water to stay long-term?

Tonight, faced with so much unknown, Ailyn became physically distraught and anxious. "Honey, I know." Ace held onto her, and they hugged each other through the tears. Sturgis came to her side, offering her comfort. He reminded her of Burr and Dock.

"Can you still feel them, Dan? Are they alive?" Ailyn asked. Desperate for reassurance that their children were alive and safe. She leaned into her husband's unusual ability to sense the unknown.

Calmly he looked down and then up again. "Actually, yeah, Honey. Yeah, I can still feel them. Both Hatty and Reese are still alive. I can feel it right here." He pointed at his heart and smiled lovingly into Ailyn's eyes.

She rebuilt her chaos inside into hope, love, and prayer for the reality her husband deeply believed in. The alternative was too difficult to manage, so, she decided that every day, she would send them her love and wait to feel it in return.

While Ace couldn't be sure they would ever see their children again, he knew hope was stronger than despair. And in order to survive, everyone in that bunker needed to maintain a positive attitude. They would need to be patient with each other and offer each other kindness and grace.

60 Minutes

Day 11, 7:11 a.m.

Minneapolis, MN

Karla and Reese moved to the interior of the Pillsbury Mill Museum after watching the darkness sweep over the horizon. They could feel everything around them shake and vibrate.

The sky was truly falling along with pieces of the buildings around them. It was becoming difficult to breathe. "Reese, do you trust me?" Karla looked deep into his fearful eyes.

"Yes."

"Follow me, and don't look back, okay."

"What about the others?"

She shook her head, grabbed his hand, and led him through a series of doorways that appeared and disappeared behind them as if through magic.

Karla led Reese down a few floors below the museum lobby. He was coughing and struggling to breathe normally. She unlocked a door with a sign that read 'Maintenance.' Once inside, she opened a metal storage closet with two portable oxygen tanks generally used by people with COPD or emphysema.

"Here, strap this over your shoulders and put the mask over your mouth. Breathe slowly and stay calm. I know you're freaking out, Reese. Slow down. Relax. Calm down, my friend, calm down. There you go, that's better!" While she spoke, her voice became calmer and more reassuring, allowing him to mirror her demeanor.

He let go of his fear and trusted her directions explicitly. Reese stopped hyperventilating and returned to a slower, softer breathing pattern. The oxygen gave him new energy, and he felt revitalized and alive.

Karla and Reese had escaped the certain death occurring above them at a horrific pace. It was probable that none of their group would survive. Nor would the majority of the country. But all that mattered to Karla was the here and now and taking shelter deep below the mill.

She took ahold of Reese's hand and led him out of the

maintenance closet, back into the hallway, and then to a doorway that read 'Stairs to Lower Level 3'.

With each new door, they descended deeper below the pending doom. The further they got below the substructure, the harder it became to forget the past. Tank air became the new normal. All of their friends just froze when the skies darkened.

Before going down, Karla practically had to drag Reese inside as the darkening skyline mesmerized him. She urgently pulled on his arm again to stay with her; he appeared to surrender, trusting her instincts.

Difficult as it was, Karla knew that only the most prepared would survive. Speaking was difficult with the mouthpieces on. Reese managed to let Karla know his headlamp was dimming. The batteries were dying.

"We're almost there. We'll use mine the rest of the way."

Karla took Reese past two signs on the locked steel entry door. One said '6th-Floor Basement', and the other said 'No Admittance-Authorized Personnel Only.' This door was roughly four feet wide and nine feet high. She searched her large ring of keys and grabbed one with a red plastic cover around its edges, sliding it into the slot and turning the key. Sounds of clicking lock tumblers and ventilator breathing was the only sounds she heard. The large door opened like a kitchen cupboard. She closed it behind them.

"Come on, Reese, almost there."

The short hallway led them to a solid wall with one of those digital keypads that required a series of coded numbers pressed in the proper sequence.

"Karla, how come you have all those keys?"

"I used to be a manager here," she replied. "Are you with me, buddy?"

A Murphy door wall suddenly opened from one side to the other. The room released a gasp of pressurized air, making a loud hissing noise when the seal broke.

"Wait until you see what I've got set up down here.

You're going to freak!" Karla's eyes displayed her excitement.

He squeezed her hand. The LED lights came to life when Karla flipped the switch.

"What is this place?" he asked, stunned at the setup.

"I know, right?!" she smiled at Reese's amazement and awe.

"Stay right here for a second. I have to shut us in and start up the hydro generator. I'll be right back."

Karla walked back toward Reese; she had removed her mask and oxygen tank. "Pretty awesome, hey?" She said with survivor enthusiasm while helping him remove his air tank.

Compared to what they had escaped above them, this was five stars! Shelving on every wall was stocked with an amazing variety of non-perishable foods. A steam shower was set up in one corner. Additionally, a stationary bike was attached to rechargeable carbon-ion batteries, allowing them to power up other necessities for long-term comfort.

"What about the others, Karla?" the words came out unfiltered.

Karla placed her hands on Reese's shoulders and said, "They're all gone, Reese, all of them, gone. We couldn't have brought anyone else with us and survived."

She moved one hand over his heart and said, "I know your heart, my friend. I know it hurts right here. I'll help you through it, okay? We'll do it together."

While Karla hadn't known the group well, she teared up. Loss of lives was always sad. Reese was also overwhelmed with emotion; the magnitude of their situation and the nation's state weighed on them both. They held onto each other and sobbed. One good cry for humanity and for those they left behind. And relief for themselves.

"Karla, thank you! Why did you pick me to come here with you? You saved my life. I think I love you!" Reese said with emotion. Karla knew their new reality would pose so many obstacles, and yet, right now, they were safe. They had plenty of time to explore their true feelings. She lightened things up, "You think so, hey?" They laughed between the tears of their new reality.

"Okay, we have to get shit done. This is our new 'home' Roomie! We need to start the filtration system to get fresh air and water."

The circuit breaker box was carefully marked and organized by color codes and written labels. Most of the circuit breakers were already on, but Karla pushed the two top breakers over, and the room started to hum.

A fan on the wall down near the floor slowly turned and delivered a soft breeze of clean, filtered air. Karla switched another fan on for the exhaust.

"Okay, I have a million questions. How did you find this place, Karla? Did you bring all of this stuff down here by yourself? How long did it take?

"We'll talk about it; we'll have plenty of time. Right now, I need you to go to the battery cells and tell me what the gauge says on top."

"It's at 75 percent."

"Okay, good. When we turned everything on, it drew about a quarter of the stored power. I'll need you to read and write the gauge percentage in this logbook every hour we're awake. Here's an egg timer. Set it for 60 minutes, and when it goes off, read the gauge, write it down, and then let me know where it's at."

"I can do that," he said back and started to organize in his mind and in their space where to put the egg timer and the logbook. He realized everything that was set up was important to their survival.

"If it goes down to fifty percent within the hour, we can calculate how often we have to recharge the cells with the bike. Reese, this won't be easy. But we will be much more comfortable while we're down here. Also, we can't let the cells die, ever; do you understand?"

"Yes!" Hey, I'm thirsty. Is there water? Do we need to ration it?"

"Well, here's the setup. The system takes groundwater from deep under the Mississippi River and filters it through a system similar to what they use in space. What we use will all get recycled too. Including our pee."

"Our pee?" Reese looked at her.

"Yup! Even our pee," she said back, giggling at the look on his face.

Karla walked Reese through how the pit latrine, floor tiles, and stationary bicycle all help generate electricity. She told him about the technologies and how they had all been refined and improved for off-grid use. A natural gas generator was there for emergencies, but eventually, the lines would empty.

It felt like, in no time at all, the egg timer went off. Reese reset the timer and read the gauge. "It's sitting between five-eighths and three-quarters!"

"No way, that's awesome!" It's more efficient than I thought it would be. Did you write that down in the logbook yet?" Her back was to him as she was reviewing the food stores.

"Yes, and will it be my job the whole time we are here? Not that I'm complaining, just curious?"

"No, sometimes I'll do it too, but we have to establish routines that follow a schedule. Wait until it's your turn to recharge the batteries. I think it will take about two hours of ride time to get a full charge if they're at fifty percent."

"It'll be a good way to stay fit for what's to come later," Reese answered, flirting with her.

"Really? I've thought about that too. Not an ideal time to start a new family." Karla opened the nightstand and held up a box of condoms.

"You've thought about everything! - They laughed again. "If I'm to be responsible for repopulating the earth, I'll do my best, if that's what I need to do!" It provided some levity when so much responsibility sat on their shoulders just to stay alive.

After a few hours of making sure everything was operational, the "empty nesters" took time to eat and talk—so many unanswered questions.

"Have you thought about your family and friends, Karla?"

"I know my Mom, Dad, and little brother are all okay. My parents have been prepping since before I was born."

"Where are you from?"

"The Minneapolis area originally. My great-great-grandfather was Charles Pillsbury. He built this mill and founded Pillsbury Flour."

"So, you are Karla Pillsbury, a descendant of C.A. Pillsbury?" he said, surprised at his girlfriend's ancestry.

"Yeah, that's me. My family is safe just north of Dallas, Texas. Dad spent millions of dollars on his bunker. He didn't want me to live here, but after I left the service, I wanted to live on my own. I changed my last name and got a job as a tour guide in the mill. Dad found out, and we built this together when he came up for visits. We've been working on this on and off over the last ten years. Really, about the time when Mrung got elected President. Dad didn't trust the political dynamics and questioned the government's motives. He wanted to make sure I had a plan up here in case anything happened. I'm glad I didn't disagree or argue with him about it, or we wouldn't be here right now."

"That's amazing, Karla. I wondered why you had all the keys and knew exactly where to go."

"How about your family?" Karla had avoided the subject earlier, concerned that the conversation might be difficult for Reese.

"Well," he paused, and his demeanor changed; "If I know my dad, he and my mom are hunkered down in an underground bunker just downriver near La Crosse,

Wisconsin. He's always talked about the end times. He told me he and Mom would go to their friend's house if we ever experienced an apocalyptic event. He taught me about survival over the years, but I didn't take it seriously. I'm not positive that they are okay. But yesterday, when we went up the ladder over the wall to go to that store on Hennepin, I had a really bizarre feeling that they were both alive. I could see them lying on the ground together, holding hands, and my mom talked to me like I was right there. So, I'm pretty sure they are okay and are underground too. But I'm not sure about my sister and her family. I can't tell if she's alright or not."

"Reese, I am a huge believer in odd and peculiar things. We can try to make mental contact with them, just like they did with you. Do you want to try?"

"Yeah, can we eat something first, though? I'm starving!"

****

Karla held Reese's hand as they lay beside each other on their new bed. Was it destiny or maybe karma that she ended up with him? It would have been so difficult to experience this alone, but being with the wrong person would be worse. She felt very comfortable and at ease with Reese; you just know when you find your person.

"Let's close our eyes," she said, speaking softly. "I'll try and guide us to them; just trust me. Think about your Mom. Imagine you are with her. Feel her in your heart. See her where she is right now. Start talking to her in your mind. I'm right there with you."

Karla felt Reese squeeze her hand, and she knew that he had made contact.

She found herself with him in a strange place, surrounded by new faces. Karla smiled an acknowledgment to the two couples and nodded her head. She knew right away which couple was Reese's parents. She saw relief and happiness as Reese's mom felt that Reese was safe and that he wasn't alone. She reached out her hand, touched the side of her face, and smiled with love. Words spoke through Karla's mind, "Your son is alive with me, and he made it through the beginning of this newly altered world. What is unknown will stay that way for a very long time. We will become one."

Reese's eyes opened. Karla had been watching him for some time. He reached for her, and they embraced, and he cried in her arms. "Thank you, Karla, thank you. I was with them and talked with my mom. Everything's going to be alright!"

"I met your parents Reese and another couple in the room. Your Mom and Dad love you very much." He cried again and held her.

"She asked me your name, and I told her I love you. It made her so happy. Thank you!"

"I love you too, Reese. We can do this! Speaking of doing this, I have to check the gauges once more before we go to bed. I'll be right back."

Karla set another alarm to go off in four hours. The power levels were still up at five-eighths. Hopefully, they would read around fifty percent to justify a few more hours of sleep before they needed to recharge the batteries.

They were both exhausted physically, mentally, and emotionally. As Karla got back into bed, she saw that Reese was already in dreamland. She turned off the LED lights and cuddled up next to him. Within minutes she, too, was fast asleep next to her new companion.

Green Revolution

Day 11, 7:27 a.m.

New Elmar, WI

"Darin, come look at this!" Hatty yelled; she was standing outside the kitchen door, looking to the west.

Stepping out the garage bay door, Darin saw a black sky looming as if God himself was holding a darkened sheet across the horizon line.

"Kids, grab your backpacks and get in the truck. Now!" Darin yelled. His tone didn't give them leeway to argue or disagree.

The ground started vibrating and shaking. Everyone jumped inside the truck, and Darin drove over the lawn to Josh and Penny's house, where they were standing on their back deck, watching. The blackness was rolling closer, enveloping everything in its path.

As Darin pulled up in his gray Dodge Power Wagon, they grabbed their bug-out bags and jumped into the back of the truck box. Darin spun grass off the manicured lawn onto the road.

Abe said, "Look!" Pointing his finger at the farm just outside of town. Darin watched as the blue Harvester silo was covered by smoke and flying debris, and then, it completely disappeared. The air was thick; everyone tried to cover their faces as they coughed and choked.

Hitting the button of a garage door opener on the visor, they watched as the ground slid sideways on the hill's edge. Darin drove his truck into the open bay door. Annie yelled for the dogs. They were catching up as they had tried to run alongside. Luckily, none were hurt by the debris. As they ran in, Darin closed the airtight entrance door behind them, blocking out the chaos. He jumped out of the vehicle and started to work on activating the bunker's lifesaving technologies.

Before the power grid failure, the bunker hadn't been opened since Grandpa Gene had passed. But when things began to feel imminent, Darin and Hatty revitalized the shelter's capabilities to accommodate their needs.

The bunker's existence had been kept secret, even from Hatty's family. Darin's father had built it to hold seven people, large by survival standards but not so large when their beloved town was being destroyed. Father Brillion and the rest of New Elmar were left unprotected.

Darin began to involve everyone in the process of preparing the bunker so they could stay safe. "Abe, turn on the air exchanger for me!"

Darin had shown Hatty what she needed to do upon arrival. She opened another door leading her down a narrow hallway deep into the hillside sanctuary. She got to another doorway that opened to the main living area of the shelter.

Darin had followed after her, and she turned to his embrace. "We made it, Hatty; we're going to be okay."

The rest of the group entered the room and closed the door behind them.

Built-in recessed wall shelving lined most of the open spaces with supplies and non-perishable food.

The adjacent room had seven-fold-down sleeping cots attached to the back walls. Privacy was now a thing of the past. Four stationary bicycles, an elliptical, and a treadmill, were in another corner, all hooked up to a 'Green Revolution' charging system for the battery banks. Fresh air filtered from his dad's hydration storage unit built into the water aquifer deep below the limestone shelf. A technology that revolutionized underground prepping after 2022. It was his dad's final accomplishment in the bunker before he passed.

'*Thank you, Dad,*' Darin thought to himself. Without this, they wouldn't be able to live underground for an extended period of time.

Darin shared how some of these things worked, what it would look like to keep the energy stores adequate, and they discussed ways to divide the various tasks everyone would have to share. Seven people are personalities with seven sets of ideas and moods every day. This would be a challenge for everyone. Staying alive was conditional on personal sacrifice. Darin didn't overwhelm everyone with everything on this first day. And he didn't share all of the shelter's features. One very unique feature he'd helped his father install was a manually operated periscope allowing them to look topside visually. He decided it best to keep this to himself, fearing the present-time nightmare of what might be seen outside on the first day.

Unfired ICBMs

Day 11, 6:13 a.m.

Norad Mountain, ID

The explosions shook the depths of the Norad sanctuary. Its inhabitants stopped, tucked, and rolled beneath any available structure sturdy enough to withstand the pressure of falling electrical fixtures and debris.

The lighting went dead upon impact. Survivors were left in pitch-black darkness and fear.

Everyone in the sanctuary dwelling heard the deafening sounds of concrete and steel expanding and contracting under immense pressure. The nuclear blasts had caused the earth's surface to implode.

Fission chain reactions utilized the hidden silos of eastern Montana, like the barrels of guns, which boosted deadly fusion plutonium warheads from unfired ICBMs stored safely underground since the seventies.

Two giant mushroom clouds rose from the earth, expanding vertically, enveloping the clear blue sky, turning it the color of ash, and blocking out the sun.

Seismic tremors rippled across the ground from the impact site, destroying everything in their path. The blast shook the entire continent; fault lines became unstable. Earthquakes along the San Andreas fault lines on the western coast devastated landscapes and caused cities to fall.

Tidal waves developed, building in strength, working their way west, impacting the eastern coastal regions of Asia and Australia.

Everyone at ground zero and within a twenty-mile radius of the blast site instantly vaporized as the air imploded, followed by incinerating fire, hurricane-force winds, and flying debris.

Wind currents moved the growing mountain of blown ash and fire eastward, leaving a burnt path of destruction to the Eastern coastline and beyond.

Some form of manufactured biological agent grew from within. Unless prepared for this disaster, inhabitants above ground suffered an agonizing death.

With over 358 million citizens in the United States and

Canada, more than 260 million perished.

Survivors, alone, cut off from aid, their government was in chaos. The country was left vulnerable to attack, ripe for the picking by any number of adversaries with less than honorable intent.

Only time would tell how the US and Canada would emerge. A once-booming superpower, the United States of America, has fallen.

Hyper-speed

Day 11, 8:11 a.m.

U.S. Virgin Islands

Regina and Alex Putman sat on their friend's sunny veranda, enjoying mimosas. Each with a half-eaten slice of bacon, egg, and cheese quiche elegantly plated before them.

The table began to tremble, and the silverware moved slowly across the glass.

Looking over at each other in surprise, Alex asked. "What the hell was that? An earthquake?"

"That, my dear husband, is my way of flipping America the middle finger. Don't worry, darling. Everything is different now, and we will live like royalty." She laughed until something odd caught her eye.

"I don't want to know, Regina. I don't want to know." Alex shook his head. Her ambitions and ideas exceeded the bounds of his simple imagination. He raised another piece of quiche to his mouth.

The trembling stopped, and life continued for the Putmans.

****

Ace stood next to the table inside the underground bunker. He broke into a cold sweat and suddenly felt faint. "Ailyn, help me!"

Ailyn screamed as her husband fell to the floor. She and Mike ran to his side and rolled him onto his back. His breath was shallow. Mike felt Ace's carotid artery; luckily, his pulse was fast and strong.

Sue grabbed a blanket and gently laid it over him. "Seizure? Heart attack?"

Ace started to lose consciousness. Everything went black, and then he saw a multi-colored spectrum of rainbow colors.

He looked down from the bunker's ceiling to see Ailyn, Mike, and Sue kneeling around his body. He tried to call out to them, but his voice didn't reach them, and he kept floating upward and away from the room. He didn't have control. He couldn't stop. He took one last look down. He entered the stratosphere seeing the earth's size shrink further as he was drawn away.

In no time, he stopped and descended. He was face-to-face with Regina Putman. She was sitting at a table with her husband, Alex, toasting a champagne glass.

She was overjoyed and exuberantly elated. She glanced casually, making eye contact, and then stopped laughing. Looking directly into Ace's eyes.

Then, suddenly Ace took a large deep inhale and sat upright.

"Oh, my God. Are you okay, Dan?" Ailyn grabbed him and hugged him, not wanting to let go.

"It was Regina Putman!" Ace said out loud.

They all looked at him, perplexed and speechless. "What?" asked Mike.

"Regina Putman caused all of this!"

"How?" Mike asked.

"I'm not sure exactly."

"No, how do you know she had anything to do with it?"

"I can't explain it, but somehow we have to stop her."

Confused, Mike scratched his head, not sure what to say next. "Take a deep breath, Ace; calm down."

Okay, yeah, it's okay, Mike. Give me a second, I can't explain what happened." Ace knew if he tried, like in the past, in middle school, everyone would think he was crazy.

Ailyn hit Ace in the shoulder with a slightly raised voice and said, "I thought you were having another heart attack. You scared the hell out of me. Don't ever do that again, you bastard!" She got up, went across the room to the sink basin, and drew a glass of water. Sue followed her and placed her arm around her living companion' shoulder to console her.

"Sorry Mike, I can't explain what happened." Ace knew he had experienced some sort of out-of-body experience. He didn't dare try to explain this to the others. Just one more strange phenomenon he once heard his grandmother talk about.

Ace, couldn't stop thinking about it and he knew when

the time was right, answers would come.

Spending the rest of the day making their new home fully functional and organized kept everyone busy. They all seemed to dismiss the strange experience and chose to move forward.

Would they have enough food and supplies to survive until it was safe to go outside?

In the midst of the apocalypse, Ace sensed few would survive. Those who live will feel pain, grief, and unprecedented loss. Some relationships will fail and falter. Others will blossom and grow. No one knew who else lived underground and when they would emerge. Only time will tell.

"Humanity's only chance for long-term survival is if the world starts making decisions based on love, not hate, power, or selfish greed."

Dana B. Auer

ABOUT THE AUTHOR

Dana B. Auer grew up the youngest of five boys on a rural hobby farm in Eastern Wisconsin, where he learned basic skills of country living and survival passed down from a family history of hard work and living.

3:33am, is his debut novella.

A husband and father, he now lives in Western Wisconsin.

Made in the USA
Monee, IL
23 March 2024

55621269R00098